More adventures of Homer Price
CENTERBURG TALES
Robert McCloskey

Centerburg *might* be your town, but there's a delightful difference—Homer Price, Dulcy Dooner, Uncle Ulysses, the flustered sheriff, and the pompous judge all live there. And that's why in Centerburg, along with the routine of small-town life, the most preposterous things keep happening.

A mad scientist grows ragweed taller than fire ladders, a jukebox gone wild sets a whole town dancing, and a slick salesman dupes the citizenry with "Ever So Much More So" magic elixir. But nothing fazes Homer Price! He solves these problems with a good supply of common sense—and ingenuity.

CENTERBURG TALES

BY ROBERT McCLOSKEY

Puffin Books

PUFFIN BOOKS
Published by the Penguin Group
Penguin Putnam Inc., 375 Hudson Street, New York, New York 10014, U.S.A.
Penguin Books Ltd, 27 Wrights Lane, London W8 5TZ, England
Penguin Books Australia Ltd, Ringwood, Victoria, Australia
Penguin Books Canada Ltd, 10 Alcorn Avenue, Toronto, Ontario, Canada M4V 3B2
Penguin Books (N.Z.) Ltd, 182–190 Wairau Road, Auckland 10, New Zealand

Penguin Books Ltd, Registered Offices: Harmondsworth, Middlesex, England

First published by The Viking Press 1951
Published in Puffin Books 1977
20

Library of Congress Cataloging in Publication Data
McCloskey, Robert.   Centerburg tales.
Reprint of the ed. published by The Viking Press, New York.
Summary: Further adventures of Homer Price, including
those in which a juke box sets the whole town singing
against its will and in which a mad scientist develops
weeds that overrun the town.
[1. Humorous stories. 2. Short stories] I. Title.
PZ7.M1336Ce 1977   [Fic]   77-21458
ISBN 0-14-031072-x

Printed in the United States of America

Set in Times Roman

CONTENTS

GRANDPA
HERCULES

I. THE HIDE-A-RIDE

IN EVERY town there is a best place to do everything. For playing marbles there is no place in the town of Centerburg as good as the alley behind the barbershop. For playing baseball the best place is the empty lot next to the Enders Products Company. This place is no good for flying kites though, because there are too many wires in the way. The best place to eat doughnuts is in Uncle Ulysses' lunchroom. The best place for ice-cream cones is Umpfschneider's Drugstore. There are lots of places where you can go fishing, but the really best place is in Curbstone Creek, just below the railroad bridge. The best place for spinning tops is the cement walk around the G.A.R. monument in the middle of the town square. Of course there are usually a lot of girls getting in the way, because that's the best place in Centerburg to play jacks and jump rope too. If you are a really expert top spinner you can make your top go hop, hop, hop, spinning right down the monument steps, providing there are no jacks players in the way.

"Homer Price, the next time you spin that top in our jacks game we'll take your top and keep it!" cried Ginny Lee. "We were here under the soldier first. You boys stay on the other side with the sailor and spin your old tops!"

"It was an accident," said Homer. "I didn't mean to spin it in your jacks."

"Yeah," said Freddy, "Homer's top just sort of glanced off the cannonballs and bounced clear around the monument."

"Homer Price, you glanced that top on purpose!" said Ginny Lee. She stood up and prepared to throw Homer's top as far as she could throw it.

"Look who's coming!" said Freddy, pointing across the town square.

"Why, it's Homer's Grandfather Hercules!" said Ginny Lee, forgetting to throw the top.

"That's him all right," said Homer, recognizing the tall old man walking swiftly in their direction.

"Nobody else around here can walk that fast," said Freddy.

"He's pretty fast, considering his age," Homer agreed. "But he says that he can't walk near so fast as he could when he was young."

"How old *is* Grampa Herc?" asked Freddy. "You can't tell whether he's *fifty* or *ninety,* to look at him."

"Grampa Herc says that he stopped counting birthdays at ninety-nine, but you know how he is, it's hard to tell when he's telling one of his stories and when he's telling what is really so."

"Do you s'pose he would tell us a story today, Homer?" asked Ginny.

"Something always reminds Grampa Herc of a story," Homer said. "And if nobody interrupts him, I expect he'll tell one."

"Wu-a-ll!" exclaimed Grampa Herc as he came gliding up to the monument. "G'mornin', girls and boys."

"Good morning, Grampa Herc," Homer greeted.

"Hello, Grampa Herc," said Freddy.

"Tell us a story, Grampa Herc," Ginny pleaded. And almost at once all of the girls and boys were gathered around Grampa Herc, demanding a story.

"Hadn't no intention of bustin' in on you young uns ball bouncin', and rope jumpin', and top spinnin'," said the old man as he took a seat on the steps and drew up his long legs. "Where did all these fancy balls and tops come from?"

"They were free," said Ginny Lee, displaying her ball and jacks.

"For nothing!" added Freddy. "From Whoopsy-Doodles!"

Grampa Hercules cupped his hand behind his good ear to make sure that he had heard right, so Homer explained, "From the Whoopsy-Doodle Breakfast Food Company, Grampa Herc. You mail in the top of a box of Whoopsy-Doodle Breakfast Food with your name written on it, and by return mail they send you a ball and jacks or a top."

"Oh, I see," said Grampa Hercules. "You buy these Whoopsy-Doodles at the grocery store to get the box tops?"

"Nope," answered Homer. "Uncle Ulysses bought a large supply of Whoopsy-Doodles for his lunchroom and there were just enough box tops for everybody."

"I remember," said Grampa Hercules, "as how one time I saved up enough plugs from chewing tobacco to send in and get a music box. Played awfully pretty music," he said, stroking his chin thoughtfully.

All the children were watching Grampa Herc closely, and they knew when he stroked his chin, in just that way, he was thinking of a story.

"Does the music box remind you of a story?" asked Ginny Lee impatiently.

"Can't say as it does," said Grampa Herc.

"Mebbe chewing tobacco plugs?" suggested Freddy hopefully.

"Nope." said Grampa Herc. "But all this bouncin' and spinnin' reminds me of something." The old man continued to stroke his wrinkled chin thoughtfully while the children seated themselves on the steps to listen.

"It was back in the days—oh, about the time Ohio was admitted to the Union or thereabouts. I was a young fella, 'bout the age of Homer here, and was just comin' to settle in the new state with my father and my uncle and a few cousins. We'd left the womenfolk back near Philadelphia until we could get ourselves settled and a few acres of land cleared. On account of how most of our new neighbors were going to be Indians, we kinda thought it would be a good idea to get acquainted before we brought the women. We come over the mountains on foot and then built ourselves a raft of logs, thinking we'd make our way down a creek and pick out a nice spot to settle somewhere along the bank. We drifted along downstream for a day or so, and then one morning our raft stopped plumb still. Thought right away we'd fetched up on a rock or a snag, but after we'd poked around with the poles we found it wasn't that. Come to find out, there was a bump in the creek, runnin' clear across and about the height of one of these steps here. Our raft was fetched up against it, and the current was pushing it so hard we couldn't budge it. Well, we all got out and took buckets and commenced to dip water from the

top of the bump and slosh it upstream to the low side, and I guess we must have put in a whole day dipping and a-sloshing and trying to level off that bump in the creek. 'Twasn't no use though, 'cause the water kept runnin' right back downstream and making the bump just as high as ever. There didn't seem to be a thing that we could do to get the raft up and over that there bump. My cousins went downstream a piece, on the other side of the bump, and built another raft. They decided that they would drift on down toward the Ohio River, but my father decided as how this place was prob'bly as good as any other, so we stayed right here.

"We built ourselves a little cabin at the top of the hill—you prob'bly all seen the spot, right there where the old canal branches out of Curbstone Creek. They built that canal a few years later, just to get boats around that bump. O' course you can't see the bump today, after all these years, unless the water is high; and even then you can scarcely notice it if the light isn't just right and reflecting off the edge. The last big flood 'bout twenty years ago, the water washed out almost all trace of that bump."

Grampa Hercules paused and stroked his whiskers thoughtfully and then repeated, "Washed out almost all trace o' that bump!"

"How about the spinning and bouncing?" asked Freddy.

"Oh, yes," said Grampa Hercules, slapping his long leg, "I'm coming to that." He pointed a long finger at Freddy and said, "Now don't you go interrupting me, young fella."

"Freddy was just reminding you, Grampa Herc," said Homer. "He wasn't trying to interrupt."

"Let's see now," said Grampa Herc, stroking his chin. "Oh, yes, spinning. Wu-a-ll," he began, "the land hereabouts turned out to be pretty good, and it got settled pretty fast, in spite o' trouble with the Indians. 'Twasn't long afore there were a lot o' little backwoods farms all up and down the creek. Most of the settlers sent their pork and wheat and maple syrup down the creek to the Ohio River and on to New Orleans to sell. Seeing as how all the flatboats for New Orleans had to start on the other side of the bump in Curbstone Creek, our little place on the hill next to the bump got to be sort of a loading and shipping center for these parts.

"There got to be a big demand for barrels to ship salt pork in, and so my father and me, we started makin' barrels. We built up a good business in barrels there on top of the hill. Then one morning—I fergit now whether it was at the time of the Great Elixer Indian Uprising or just after the Curbstone Creek Uprising—we were goin' about our business, cuttin' staves and bendin' barrel hoops, when I just by accident happened to glance up at one of the barrels we had finished the day before. I noticed the tip of a feather sticking up from the inside! It sent a chill down my spine, because I figgered there was an Indian on the other end of that feather, waiting in that barrel to add a few scalps to his belt. I motioned to my father, and he quick as a wink slammed a top on the barrel and sat on it while I nailed it down tight. We had ourselves a barreled Indian, a-thumpin' and yellin' fit to kill!"

Grampa Herc paused to chuckle and stroke his chin, then he

17

went on, "We decided we'd send him off to New Orleans on the next flatboat, and we went back to our work of making barrels. I kept thinking to myself how surprised somebody was going to be when he opened that barrel and found that he had himself an Indian instead of a side o' pork. That Indian was thumpin' around and rockin' the barrel while we got along with our work. We laughed an didn't pay much attention, until there was an extra loud thump! We looked up just in time to see the barrel tip over on its side and start rollin' down the hill! Wu-a-ll! I tell you, that barrel o' Indian went a-spinnin' and bouncin' and jumpin' down that hill like a bolt o' lightning. It smacked up agin that old sycamore tree right on the bank of the creek, and the barrel— it was a strong barrel too—smashed all to kindling. I declare, some o' the pieces wasn't any bigger'n a splinter.

"Heh, heh!" Grampa Herc paused to giggle and then continued, "And that there Indian bounced right into Curbstone Creek! We

laughed and laughed, just couldn't help ourselves, even though we were sorta worried for fear that this might touch off another mess of trouble with the Indians. That was the saddest-looking Indian I ever did see, came a-sputterin' and drippin' out of the creek, and lit off into the woods.

"Wu-a-ll! We thought sure we were in for it the next morning! There were *two* feathers, stickin' out o' *two* barrels, but, by gorry, we worked the same stunt on 'em and nailed 'em up tight, jist like the first Indian, and durned if *they* didn't manage to tip the barrels and go spinning down the hill and smack up agin the old sycamore on the bank. Both Indians bounced into Curbstone Creek, same's before. Wu-a-ll! Do you know, it got so every morning we had to nail up a couple of these fellas and roll 'em down the hill before we could commence work? Come to find out, that first Indian had gone back to the tribe and bragged about spinning around in that barrel, and how dizzy it made him feel. O' course all the other braves had to try it too, and it got to be sort of a distinction in the tribe. Got so it was hard for us to get on with our work, with these Redskins hanging around, begging to be rolled down the hill in a barrel. It finally got to where we couldn't even make enough barrels to fill the need for rolling Indians! The pile o' broken barrels around the old sycamore was getting higher and higher, and so my father finally hit on an idea. We built this extra-strong barrel and rigged it up on an axle; then we took some rawhide belts and hooked the thing onto our windmill. I declare, it was the gosh-awfullest-looking contraption I ever did see, but, by

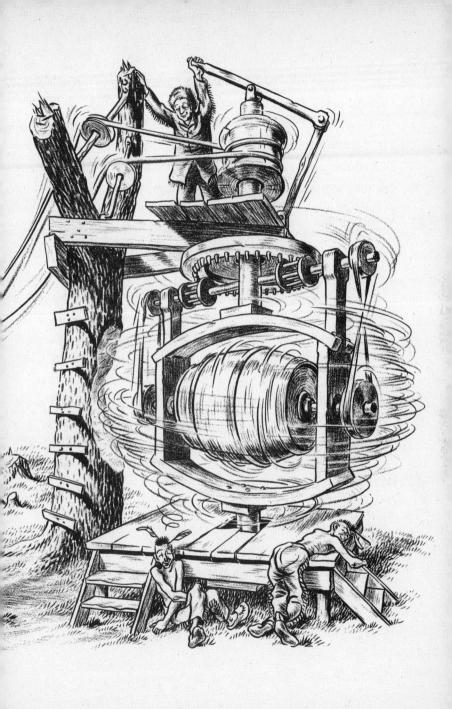

gorry, it worked! When the wind blew and my father threw in the clutch, that barrel commenced to spin just as pretty as a top. Wu-a-ll! We started charging the Indians a buffalo hide for a spin in this contraption, and it got to be known as the Hide-a-Ride. Of course we'd accept *any* kind of skins or pelts—fox, beaver, skunk, and mink. 'Twasn't long before we were sendin' *bales* of skins out of here. On a calm day sometimes there'd be as many as five, six hundred Indians standing in line, waiting and praying for the wind to blow, and blow hard, so's they could get good and dizzy inside that Hide-a-Ride.

"O' course we added a few improvements, like dousing the customer with a bucket of water when he stepped out of the machine—just to take the place of ducking in Curbstone Creek, you see—because the Indians felt they wasn't gettin' their hide's worth if they didn't get good and wet besides being dizzy.

"Those Redskins would rather have gone for a spin in the Hide-a-Ride than eat," said Grampa Hercules, stretching his long legs and getting to his feet. "And mentioning sumpthin to eat, let's all of us get on over to Ulysses' lunchroom, and I'll buy everybody a doughnut."

Grampa Hercules strode off toward the lunchroom at a good fast pace, with all the children tagging along, almost having to run to keep up.

"Wu-a-ll!" cried Grampa Hercules, flinging open the door of the lunchroom with a flick of his long arm. "Howdee-doo, Ulysses. G'd afternoon, Sheriff. Put aside that old checkers game and come and wait on these customers," he demanded, indicating the noisy group of boys and girls pouring through the door.

"Howdy, Grampa Herc," said Uncle Ulysses. "Betcha you been tellin' some of those tall tales of yours."

"Hercules," said the sheriff, "don't you ever get tired of tellin' those stories?"

"O' course not," said Grampa Hercules. "Why, I remember, Sheriff, when you and Ulysses both were little minnows, scarce big enough to fry, sittin' on the monument steps, listenin' to my stories. Pass around the doughnuts, Ulysses," said Grampa Herc, thumping on the counter. "I declare, you're getting slower every day. Not enough exercise, I reckon, because of all these fancy doodads to do the work for you." Grampa Hercules took a handful of doughnuts off the plate that Uncle Ulysses was passing around and said, "Much obliged, Ulysses," and then he turned to the children and said, "Step right up and help yourselves, young uns."

"Wouldn't you children all like a nice big bowl of Whoopsy-Doodles to eat with your doughnuts?" Uncle Ulysses offered.

There was a loud chorus of *"No!"* from the boys, and a few of the girls remembered to say, "No, thank you."

Uncle Ulysses wagged his head sadly. "What will I ever do with six dozen boxes of Whoopsy-Doodles? Seventy-two boxes without tops, gettin' staler every day, and not one of my customers likes 'em, even when they're fresh!"

"Tell you what, Ulysses," said Grampa Herc. "My chickens

23

are not finicky about what they have for breakfast, so I'll feed your six dozen boxes of stale Whoopsy-Doodles to the hens, and bring you a dozen eggs in exchange."

"It's a deal," said Uncle Ulysses. "Last year I had to throw out seventy-two boxes of Wheatsy-Beatsys."

"I remember," growled the sheriff. "And all of you young uns was shootin' up the town with yer Wheatsy-Beatsy Ray Guns! Every time I turned around, an Eastsy-Wheatsy Gay Run anged off in my beer—I mean ear!"

"Aren't you ashamed," Grampa Herc asked the children with a grin, "frightenin' the law like that?"

"Now, Hercules!" shouted the sheriff, "I—"

"I was thinkin' of you just yesterday, Grampa Hercules," said Uncle Ulysses, quickly changing the subject to avoid a quarrel. "I was looking at one of those old magazines over in the barbershop, and run across a picture of a man carrying a full-grown bull on his back."

"Wu-a-ll," said Grampa Hercules, "that's an old, old stunt of mine. All of us old-timers used to do it all the time! You start a-liftin' the critter when he's just a calf, and keep on liftin' him every day. The critter keeps growin' an gettin' bigger an heavier every day, and first thing you know, yer liftin' a mighty big hunk of animal, and it don't seem like nothing at all!

"Ulysses, 're you keepin' count of how many doughnuts we're eatin'?" he asked. Then he turned to the children. "Now don't be bashful, young uns, help yourselves. Lifting a horse," he continued, "wu-a-ll, a horse is a sure enough hard thing to lift. 'Tisn't that he's so heavy, but the critter's feet keep getting in the way. It takes a mighty tall man to walk up to a horse and pick 'im up off the ground. In the early days I was the only fellow in this corner of the state tall enough to turn the trick. There were plenty o' men around in those days who could stand on a *stump* and get a horse up across their shoulders, but I was the only one who could do it with my feet on the *ground*. That brings to mind the winter that Jeb Enders and me were hauling salt down to Cincinnati.

"We had a two-horse team, and our wagon was loaded down for a fare-you-well—lot more than we should oughta been carrying. Wu-a-ll! We was makin' our way as best we could on this old worn-out plank road when we came to a bridge. We took one look at the old thing and knew right away that it wasn't strong enough to hold up our heavy outfit. 'Herc,' says Jeb, 'there's ice on that creek, so let's work the wagon across the ice.' But I said, 'Jeb, that ice isn't strong enough to hold up the horses, let alone the load o' salt. The critters will poke right through that ice and break a leg. I tell you what I'll do; I'll stand down there on the ice underneath the bridge and brace myself so's to hold the old thing up while you drive across.' Wu-a-ll! I got down there on the ice and braced myself and got my back up against those old timbers. 'Giddap!' says Jeb, and our outfit starts rumbling

across the bridge. The old timbers creaked and groaned, but I held up the whole shebang. A team o' horses, and a wagonload o' salt, and Jeb too—he wasn't what you'd call a milkweed pod, weighed two hundred or thereabouts."

"Look here, Grampa Herc," Uncle Ulysses interrupted, "I've been wondering for thirty years, since you first told me that story, why didn't *your* feet poke through the ice with all that weight pushing down on you?"

"Yeah, Hercules," said the sheriff, chuckling, "that's been worryin' me for years too."

"Now you fellas stop makin' remarks and interruptin' my story," shouted Grampa Hercules. "Don't give a fella a chance to finish what he's sayin'," he grumbled. *"O' course* my feet poked through the ice when the wagon was just about halfway across the bridge, and I had to tread water till the dadblamed thing got to the other side.

"That water was cold as a well-digger's ankle too! I came thrashin' my way out of the creek, and Jeb built up a fire for me to dry my boots and clothes before they froze stiff. Wu-a-ll, I pulled off my boots, and do you know, there was a couple of nice catfish, one in each boot! We sat down and ate 'em right there, while we waited for my clothes to dry."

"Hold on, Hercules!" shouted the sheriff, over the laughing of the girls and boys. "You're changing the ending!"

"Yeah," said Uncle Ulysses, "that's not the way you told it when I was a boy."

"O' course not," Grampa Hercules defended himself. "That story keeps getting older and changing every year, just like people. The trouble with you fellas is not enough exercise. You're getting older and losing your sense of humor, and this story keeps getting older and better!"

"Now don't get mad, Hercules," pleaded the sheriff. "We were just curious, that's all!"

"We didn't mean any harm," said Uncle Ulysses. "Here, everybody have another doughnut on the house," he urged. "You go right ahead and tell that story just the way you want, Grampa Herc. The customer is always right, I always say. The customer is always right!"

II. SPARROW COURTHOUSE

Everybody had another doughnut, and Grampa Herc calmed down. Uncle Ulysses was relieved, and so was the sheriff. Their concerned expressions showed that they were thinking of the last time Grampa Herc really got mad.

"Did you finally get the load of salt to Cincinnati, Grampa Herc?" asked Ginny Lee.

"Wu-a-ll," said the old man, "after I got my clothes dry, and Jeb and me had finished the last of our catfish, we set out down the road again. That old road wound itself among the hills and down through East Mortonsberg and on down through Sparrow Courthouse. Now Sparrow Courthouse, there was a town for you!" Grampa Herc chuckled. "The folks in that town were always putting on airs, tried to get their town made the capital of the state and the county seat! I declare, the whole population of the town was only about four families and about forty thousand sparrows! Wu-a-ll! Like I said, these folks were always putting on airs. They built the main street of the town wide enough for a city the size of New York, and perched their dozen or so houses and general store down both sides. And the *courthouse,* that was a sight, a-sittin' like a wedding cake at the head of that wide, muddy street. Most of us settlers used to get up with the sun and put ourselves to bed when it got dark. There was hardly a watch or a clock farther west than Philidelphy, 'ceptin' mebbe one or two in Cincinnati. Yup, we got up at the break of day, and we went to roost with the chickens, and we ate when we got hungry.

"But that wasn't good enough for a fancy town like Sparrow Courthouse. They had to have a clock in that fancy courthouse steeple of theirs—sent all the way to Europe to get the thing, and hauled it over the mountains on an oxcart. Those folks were sure proud o' that clock. They started timing everything by it. They went to bed and they got up and they ate their vittles by that clock.

"Wu-a-ll! When Jeb and me came a-draggin' into Sparrow Courthouse with our load o' salt, that fancy clock was just striking eleven. 'Jeb,' I said, 'we're coming into this place just in time for lunch.' We drove down that wide street and we noticed how the general store was closed, tight as a drum, and all the houses and the inn were closed up, with the blinds pulled down and nary a latch string hanging out; even that fancy courthouse was closed up like a scairt turtle. Jeb and me looked at each other and right off reached for our rifles, 'cause nacherly we figgered there'd been an uprising. Wu-a-ll, we got out of the wagon and commenced to go creeping around to see how things stood. By gorry, do you know that every single cussid Sparrow Courthouser was in his bed just a-sleepin' and snorin' for to beat the band! Yessiree! We knew right off that it wasn't an uprising because they all had their scalps, and if we hadn't had our minds on Indians, we'd have known better in the first place. We'd have noticed the snoring noise even over the chirping of those forty thousand sparrows.

" 'Peeculiar, mighty peeculiar,' said Jeb, and I said, 'Jeb, since we're not in any special hurry to get this salt to Cincinnati, let's stick around here for a spell and see what happens.'

"Wu-a-ll, we sat there in the wagon and waited—waited clear through the afternoon, and Jeb, he commenced to get fidgity, the peeping and chirping of all those forty thousand sparrows was getting on his nerves. But we kept on waiting, and by and by when the clock struck six we commenced to see signs o' life in the place. Folks began getting up and milking cows, hauling in wood and building fires. The inn was opening up too, so we eased ourselves over and said to the proprietor as how we would like some supper. 'Supper!' he says to us. 'Supper!' he says. 'Why, stranger, we're about to serve *breakfast!*'

" 'Oh, pshaw!' says Jeb, 'do you mean to tell me you're goin' to serve us breakfast when it's gettin' dark?'

" 'Stranger,' says the innkeeper, 'you just squint your eye up to that there courthouse clock. It's a-tickin' and a-tockin' right on towards eight o'clock in the morning. Look,' he says, 'there're the young uns making for the little red schoolhouse.'

"That innkeeper looked at us as if he thought we were crazy, and we were almost beginning to allow as how he might be right. But, being hungry, we didn't argue with the fella. We ate some of his ham and eggs before we got around to asking him how it come to pass it's nine o'clock in the morning at Sparrow Courthouse, and there it was, getting dark as a licorice stick in a satchel of soot outside.

" 'My friends,' he says, ' 'twasn't until shortly after we got this wonderful clock that we folks began to realize what an unusual spot we are living in. It's nigh onto four months now since we first noticed that it was getting dark earlier every day, and getting light earlier every morning. After a couple of months it was getting dark somewheres around noon, and daybreak put in its appearance in the middle of the night. My friends,' he says, 'the sun has gradually worked its way around to setting every morning, and rising come evening!'

" 'Peeculiar,' says Jeb. 'Mighty peeculiar, because the sun don't go cuttin' up that way in any other corner o' the state of Ohio.'

" 'Naturally not, because this is an amazing feenomina!' says the innkeeper, sort of putting on airs, 'and Sparrow Courthouse is the *only town* in the United States that's got dark daytime and light nights! We're thinking of signing a peetition and sending it off to the President, asking him to set up the Sparrow Courthouse National Park.'

" 'Mister Innkeeper,' I said, 'if I were you, I'd sign a peetition asking to call this dark daylight of yours *night,* and this light night of yours *day!'*

" 'Yup,' says Jeb, 'it must be a considerable nuisance, havin' to keep your shades pulled tight all night to keep out the light, and to walk around with a lantern all day because of the dark.'

"Wu-a-ll, one thing led to another, and first thing we knew, we were arguing with this fellow.

"I allowed as how if I lived in Sparrow Courthouse I'd do what sleeping there was to be done in the daytime, and then get up and go about my business at night. That made him mad, it sure made him mad.

" ' 'Tain't natural to sleep in the daytime, even if it is dark!' he shouts at me.

"My dander was pretty well up by then and I shouted right back, ' 'Tain't natural to be up and skidaddling about in the dark even if it is daytime!'

" 'Oh, pshaw!' said Jeb. ' 'Tain't no use arguing with him, let's get some sleep.'

33

"Wu-a-ll, after a good spell of sleeping we got up the next evening with the sparrows a-chirping and a-peeping and the sun coming up over the hills just as pretty as all get out. I sort of had an idea thumping around inside of my head, but I waited until we ate some supper before I mentioned it.

34

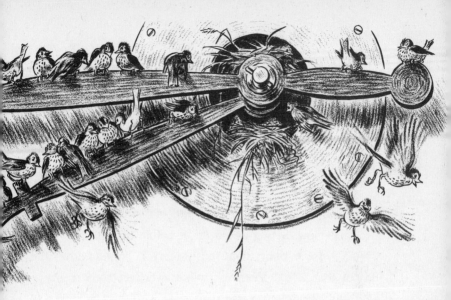

" 'Mister Innkeeper,' I said, 'I've got it all figgered out why the town of Sparrow Courthouse is having dark daylight and light night. The sun didn't go cutting didoes hereabouts until you got that fancy courthouse clock, so, the way I figger it, that clock is running *slow!*'

" 'Oh, no,' he said, 'that clock is balanced perfect, stranger. Why that clock came all the way from Europe, and we hauled it over the mountains on an oxcart! It couldn't be that clock!' he said to me, 'because the sun just gradually worked its way around to coming up a little bit earlier every day.'

" 'Look here, mister,' I said, 'something is unbalancing your fine clock from Europe that you hauled over the mountains on an oxcart. You just squint your eye up at that clock, pointing to a quarter o' eight. It's as plain as day what's discombobulating

35

the balance o' that clock. Why, that thing is no more in balance than a fat man and a feather on a teeter-totter! Just look at all those sparrows sitting on the hands and weighting 'em down, and a-holding 'em back so the poor clock can scarcely tick a tock!'

"That fellow was sure surprised. 'You get rid of those sparrows and you'll get rid of your dark daytime and light nighttime,' I said, and we hitched up an' drove off with our load o' salt, leaving him standing there with his mouth hanging open so far we were afraid a sparrow or two would fly in before he got it shut up.

"Wu-a-ll, I was right about those sparrows holding down the hands of that clock. The next winter when Jeb and I drove through Sparrow Courthouse their days were just as bright as day, and their nights were just as dark as night. The innkeeper told us that they had waited another four months after we'd told 'em what the trouble was, until the sparrows had held the clock back enough to make the days come out being day, and the nights come out being night. Then they got themselves a pair of sparrow hawks and kept 'em up in the courthouse steeple to scare away the sparrows—they haven't had a mite of dark daylight since. But do you know, those poor Sparrow Courthousers weren't out o' trouble yet! They were all worried about what under the sun could have happened to the whole day that was lost somewhere, on account of how the sparrows held back the clock. Jeb an' I told 'em to bide their time for a couple years until Leap Year came around with an extra day and that would make everything come out even."

Grampa Hercules' sharp eyes looked down the row of young faces in his audience and came to rest on the empty doughnut plate. Before he could demand another round of doughnuts Uncle Ulysses said, "Now that's another story that's been disturbing me for years."

"Oh, pshaw, Ulysses," said Grampa Hercules scornfully. "That story doesn't confuse any of you young uns, does it?" he asked the girls and boys. "See there, Ulysses, they're not confused a mite, so don't you go telling me a grown-up grandchild of mine can't see it's as plain as the nose on your face how it was the sparrows weighting down the hands of that clock! It was the sparrows that got Sparrow Courthouse all discombobulated and daytime nightwards and nightside daymost!"

"I could never figure," said Uncle Ulysses, "why it was, if the weight of the sparrows held back the hands of that clock when they were trying to tick their way up to twelve, like they are when it's quarter to eight, why didn't the weight of those sparrows push the hands down faster, when they were ticking their way down toward six, like they are at quarter past four?" Uncle Ulysses drew a diagram on a paper napkin to help explain.

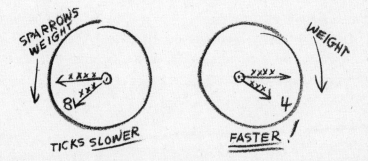

Grampa Herc sat there rubbing his chin and thinking about what Uncle Ulysses had said.

"Hercules," said the sheriff, "you'll have to admit that if you add and subtract the speight of them warrows—I mean weight of them sparrows—it would make the clock run on time!"

"There you go again, both of you!" cried Grampa Hercules. "Interrupting and making remarks and trying to ruin another story! I've been telling that story for more years than the two of you have been alive, and you're the first ones to complain and as much as tell me that I'm abusing the facts!" said Grampa Herc, rolling up his sleeves. "Them's fightin' words!"

"Mebbe the sparrows flew away to eat every half-hour, Grampa Herc," Homer suggested, trying to duck the old man's elbows.

"That would explain everything! We're sorry we mentioned it!" said the sheriff and Uncle Ulysses from under the counter.

"You two fellas," growled Grampa Herc, sitting down on his stool once more, "are just like the crazy fella eatin' a doughnut and smackin' his lips over every bite when all of a sudden he commences to worry himself into a case of indigestion over what's become of the hole in the middle!"

"Don't take on thataway, Hercules," pleaded the sheriff. "We were only trying to get straight on the finer points o' your story."

"It's mighty discouraging for a man to have his word questioned thataway," said Grampa Hercules. "A storyteller's got enough trouble on his hands nowadays trying to hold his own against Super-Dupers and rocket ships and all kinds o' newfangled truck. For two cents I'd stop telling folks about the experiences o' my younger—"

Grampa Hercules stopped short as the door opened and two strangers entered the lunchroom. "Hello, everybody!" one of them said. "This joint looks 'bout the same as ever, except you got it all cluttered up with kids!"

"Why, it's Mr. Gabby!" said Homer.

"The one and only!" said Mr. Gabby. "This is my partner, Max," he said, introducing his companion.

"Looks like the advertising business is pretty good these days, Mr. Gabby," said Uncle Ulysses.

"Yeah," said the sheriff, "we didn't recognize you dressed in those store clothes."

"Pretty classy outfit, huh?" asked Mr. Gabby, flicking a bit of dust from his sleeve. "You're looking at the new and improved Mr. Gabby in the bright new doublebreasted pin-striped package. I quit being a sandwich man in outdoor advertising. I'm an executive now. Max and me has got our own advertising company. We're experts in packaging."

"Golly, Mr. Gabby, that sounds pretty important," said Homer.

"Important!" echoed Mr. Gabby. "Why, that's one of the most important jobs there is! You see, when some company has got a new kind of soap, or toothpaste, or catsup, Max and me think up a classy-looking wrapper, or tube, or streamlined bottle to put it in, so's people will buy it."

"I can recollect when most everything was put in barrels and kegs," said Grampa Hercules. "I made a lot o' barrels and kegs in my day."

"Barrels were all right in their day," said Mr. Gabby, "but with modern advertising you can't sell stuff in barrels."

"Barrels have no eye appeal," said Max. "Nobody would dream of buying anything in a barrel in this Modern Age."

"You're absolutely, positively right," said Mr. Gabby. "Even if you wrapped a barrel in cellophane you couldn't sell nothin' in it. Besides, nobody could write their name on a barrel top and send it in to enter a prize contest or get something free."

"Do you think up prize contests too, Mr. Gabby?" asked Freddy.

" 'At's right," Mr. Gabby agreed.

"And do you think up what to give away in exchange for box tops, Mr. Gabby?" asked Homer.

" 'At's my business, sonny!" replied Mr. Gabby with a flourish. "Max," he commanded, "you tell them about Vimmy-Swimmys."

"Vimmy-Swimmys," Max said reverently, "is a brand-new kind of breakfast food!"

"The breakfast of champion swimmers!" added Mr. Gabby.

"Every bite is waterproofed!" exclaimed Max.

"And that's a fact!" confided Mr. Gabby. "They float so good that they're hard to swallow! We thunk up a swell box top for this cereal," he continued. "You send it in, and by return mail you get a pair of water wings."

"And that's not all," said Max. "You also get a pair of genuine rubber webbed feet!"

" 'Get in the swim with Vimmy-Swimmys!' " chanted Max and Mr. Gabby in perfect unison.

"That sounds like something I've heard somewhere before," said Uncle Ulysses with a frown.

"No," said Max firmly, "you have positively never heard that offer before."

" 'Cause we just thought it up yesterday," said Mr. Gabby with pride, "and the boxes and box tops are not even printed yet.

Now we're going to get *Buster Buyseps* to write an endorsement for Vimmy-Swimmys!"

"You mean Buster Buyseps, the champion swimmer who's in the movies?" asked Freddy, hardly able to believe his ears.

"That's right, sonny," said Max. "We're going to get the one and only Buster Buyseps to recommend Vimmy-Swimmys. We're on our way to have a conference with Buster and get his endorsement."

"You bet!" said Mr. Gabby proudly. "We're driving out to good old Hollywood, California, to sign up Buster for Vimmy-Swimmys!"

"Let's eat and get on our way," Max suggested impatiently. "I'll have a blue-plate special."

"Me too," Mr. Gabby ordered, and while Uncle Ulysses started dishing out two blue-plates, Mr. Gabby hummed a few measures of "California, Here I Come."

III. LOOKING FOR GOLD

"That reminds me," said Grampa Hercules, "of the experience I had out in California."

"Yeah?" Max remarked indifferently.

"Yup," said Grampa Hercules. "I spent considerable time out in California some years ago, panning for *gold!*"

"Yeah?" asked Max.

42

"Yup," continued Grampa Hercules. "Was a lot of gold in California in those days, and I reckon I found my share of it."

"Did you really find gold?" asked Max, taking a sudden interest in what was going on.

"Yer durned tootin' we found gold!" said Grampa Hercules. "We was loaded with the stuff."

"Let's hear about it, pop," said Mr. Gabby.

"Wu-a-ll," said Grampa Hercules, "it was Hopper's idea that we pack up and go scouting out west to look for gold. Hopper wasn't his real name, his real name was George, George McThud, but everybody called him by the name o' Hopper because he was so restless and always hopping around like a toad in a burr patch. Wu-a-ll, like I said, it was Hopper McThud's idea that we go out west and try our luck at panning for gold. He came up to me one day and said, 'Hercules, things are getting almighty slow hereabouts, since all them Indians are gone. Let's pack up our duds and go out west hunting for gold.'

"I was a-getting pretty fed up myself with just building barrels an' hauling salt. Centerburg was getting to be quite a town, even had a sheriff way back then. O' course he didn't have much to do, and he sat around all day playing checkers, same as now."

At this point the sheriff broke in and said, "Dadgommit, that's not so, Hercules!"

"You going to let me tell this story, Sheriff?" asked Grampa Hercules, "or do I have to—"

"Okay, okay," said Mr. Gabby impatiently, "so you and this

here Hopper guy go off to look for gold. What happened next?"

"Wu-a-ll," Grampa Hercules continued, "to make a long story short, Hopper and I went down to Cincinnati and got ourselves aboard the *Buckeye Bride*. She was an awfully pretty steamboat, one o' the finest on the Cincinnati to St. Louis run. Her smokestacks were—"

"Okay, okay, pop," Mr. Gabby interrupted again, "you can skip the commercial because we don't want to buy the boat. Let's get to the part about the gold!"

"Mister, if you knew me better you wouldn't interrupt me thataway," threatened Grampa Hercules. "It took Hopper and me three months to get out to the West Coast. To hear you carrying on, a person would think I wasn't telling this story right." Grampa Hercules looked around threateningly, then went on.

"Wu-a-ll, after three months of traveling, Hopper and me got to Californy. We bought ourselves a couple o' those little mules, and some picks and shovels and pans to pan out gold with, and a lot o' little buckskin bags to put the nuggets in. And we stocked up real good with vittles, afore we set out for the hills.

"To hear some folks talk, you'd think that findin' gold was a powerfully difficult job, but that isn't so if you know where to look for it. In Californy, you didn't even have to know where to look, all you had to do was to follow the crowd. Why, a body had to be extra careful *not* to find the blamed stuff.

"In some of those towns a fella would have to keep his fingers crossed when he built a house, or, sure as fate, gold would be discovered in his backyard; then he'd have to tear down his house and wash away his yard to get the gold out.

"Towns and settlements had already started building up around most of the workings, and such carryings on I've never seen the like of, even to this day! Since Hopper and me had come clear across the country to get away from towns for a spell, we decided we would take off for the hills and find our own place to pan for gold.

"Wu-a-ll, pretty much out to the end of nowhere, we found a nice little stream o' water, running along at the base of a high cliff. 'Hopper,' I said, 'let's stay here for a spell and set up camp by the bottom of this cliff. Something tells me there ought to be pay dirt hereabouts just waiting for us to pan it out.'

"And there *was* gold right there at the foot o' that cliff. Shucks, don't let anybody tell you that gold is hard to find. It's just as easy as rolling off a log. That yellow stuff is scattered all over the map like the spots on a speckled hen."

Grampa Herc leaned over and tapped Mr. Gabby on the arm. "In those days a man had to be an awful dull tool not to run across at least a small amount o' gold once he'd made up his mind that was what he was looking for."

Mr. Gabby looked disgusted. "Creepers, pop, that yarn of yours is about as exciting as walking upstairs. No bandits or Indians shot at you. Nobody tried to jump your claim. And you didn't even run out of water in the middle of the desert!"

"Hold on there!" cried Grampa Hercules, his voice rising to a bellow. "Stop interrupting this story! They're common everyday occurrences, what you're talking about. Shucks, fella, I've been shot at and gone hungry more times than you've been to see a moving picture show.

"It's like I said, discovering gold isn't so powerfully exciting, it's what happens to a man *after* he's discovered the stuff. It's a funny thing, I've seen a lot of men discover gold, and you can never tell just how it's going to affect 'em. Some fellows have to rush right off and spend every last bit of it, and others wanta hoard it up and see how big a pile they can get. There are others who use the gold to see how much power they can get, and they commence to throw their weight around something awful. Then every once in a while I've seen a fellow begin to wonder what

46

he's doing, digging and scratching this stuff out o' the ground, when it isn't good to eat and you can't build anything with it. Gold won't keep you warm in the wintertime like coal does, and you can't wear the stuff except in a set of store teeth or some shiny thingamabob that you might as well do without.

"That Hopper McThud now, he being such a restless fellow, I thought he'd go rushing around and spending it quick as he could, but that wasn't so at all. He turned out to be one of the hoarding kind—surprised me no end, that did! And me, I was one of the kind who couldn't hold onto it, I had to spend it fast as I panned it out.

"Wu-a-ll, we panned and we panned. Let me tell you something, mister, there's nothing exciting about *panning* gold either. All you do, all day long, is take a spadeful of dirt and toss it in your pan. Then you dip the pan in the water and commence to shake it back and forth in a way so's the gravel and the dirt washes out. You just keep on shaking back and forth, back and forth, and finally there's a gold nugget or two shining in the bottom o' the pan. Gold is powerfully heavy stuff, you see, and it sinks to the bottom instead of washing out with the dirt.

"Wu-a-ll, we sat there on our haunches on the banks of that stream, spading and dipping and a-panning. Hopper, when he'd panned himself out a nugget, would right away put it in a little buckskin bag hung on his belt. He'd fill up one little bag with nuggets and then he'd start right in filling another one. Like I said, Hopper turned out to be the hoarding kind, and he'd keep

47

a careful count of his little bags of gold. He never let those bags get off his belt either—wore them night and day, for fear somebody would swipe 'em. About that time our coffee pot sprung a leak and we couldn't use it to make coffee in, so I kept my gold in that. Every couple of weeks, when the coffee pot got full, I'd ride into town on my mule and spend every last bit of it, right down to the bottom of the pot. Then I'd come riding back to pan out another potful, and watch Hopper count his little bags hung all around his belt. The more gold Hopper panned, the more restless he got, and he hopped around more than ever. He'd pan out a few nuggets on one side of the stream and put them in one of the little bags hung on his belt; then he'd hop over to the *other* side of the stream and pan out a few more, to hoard in one of his little bags.

"Gold is mighty heavy stuff, and you could tell that Hopper's little bags of gold were beginnin' to weigh considerable, because they pulled his belt and his drawers away down on his hips so his shirt tails were always flapping out when he jumped back and forth across that little stream. Hopper's bags of gold were gradually getting *heavier* and *heavier,* but it didn't seem to bother him the least bit. He just kept on panning and hoarding and hopping, first on the cliff side of the stream and then on the other side.

"Wu-a-ll, one day I was setting there next to the little stream when all at once an idea came into my head. 'Hopper,' I calls across to him, 'this water feels mighty nice, so I think I'll take a *bath!*'

" 'What?' asked Hopper, and he looked at me as though I'd lost my senses. 'Why, we ain't been out here pannin' fer gold fer more than four months,' he said, 'and I know fer a fact you had a bath just before we left Ohio!'

"Now don't you young uns laugh at that!" Grampa Herc commanded when Homer and Freddy and Ginny Lee and all the other children snickered and giggled. "We had mighty good soap in those days. It didn't come in a fancy box or wrapper, but, by gum, when you washed something with it, that something stayed clean!"

Mr. Gabby was about to contradict Grampa Hercules, but he noticed the glint in the old man's eyes and held his peace.

" 'Yup,' I said, 'I'm going to take a bath!' And I took off my clothes and waded in. 'Come on in!' I called across to Hopper, 'the water's fine!'

"Hopper didn't say anything. He just shook his head and picked a nugget out o' the bottom o' his pan and put it in a little bag on his belt. Then he hopped across the stream and started right in panning again. I was having a good old time swishing myself around in that water and watching Hopper pan out a nugget first on one side, then hop across and pan out another nugget on the other. Then he'd edge his way upstream a mite and start all over.

" 'Hopper,' I hollered, 'I wish you'd hop downstream a mite, because you're muddying up my bath water something awful with the dirt you're washing out o' your pan!'

And Hopper, he came hopping downstream again. By gorry, that fella was restless! He came to a halt near where I was bathing and stood there watching me, shifting his weight from one foot to the other and toying with buttons on his shirt.

" 'You say the water is fine?' he asked me.

" 'It's mighty fine!' I said. 'Why don't you come on in?'

" 'Well,' said Hopper, still fidgiting around on the bank, 'I'd sort of like to, but I guess I'd better not, I might catch cold.'

"Wu-a-ll, all of a sudden it came to me what Hopper's trouble was. He was afraid to go in bathing for fear somebody would take the little bags of gold if he took off his belt for even a minute. Like I said, you can never tell how gold is going to affect a fellow, and poor Hopper, I think he was beginning not to trust even me.

"I sat myself down in the middle of the stream, facing away from him, and said, 'Hopper, I'm going to close my eyes, and I won't look until you say *ready*. You go up there in the bushes a piece and bury your belt with its bags of gold, then you can come in bathing without worrying.'

"I could hear him spading and scurrying around up there in the bushes, and then by and by he called out, 'Ready!'

"I turned around, and there came Hopper, bouncing down

to the bank without his belt. He took off his clothes and started to wade in. I couldn't tell whether the pebbles were hurting his feet, or whether he was just fidgiting, then I guess he decided he would wade in from the other side. Anyway, Hopper *hopped!* Heavens to Betsy, what a *hop* that Hopper McThud *hopped!* I sat there in the water and watched him sail through the air, going up, up, up, and land neat as a pigeon atop that cliff, three hundred feet high if it was an inch!

"Yessiree!" said Grampa Herc loudly, to make himself heard above the amazed and pleased voices of the boys and girls. "Yessiree! Hopper McThud had been hopping back and forth across that little stream for about four months, and every time he hopped, his gold that he was hoarding in his little bags was just a little bit heavier by one or two nuggets. When you work up gradually to hopping with a heavy weight like that on your belt, it sure plays hob when you take it off all at once!

"That's not all," Grampa Hercules hastened to say. "Now there's Hopper McThud perched way up there, atop a three-hundred-foot cliff that's smooth as a wall, and he just as naked as the day he was born!

"Hopper couldn't hop himself down again, and there wasn't

any way for him to climb down. About twenty miles north there was a sort o' trail that he could have come down, but he'd have been awfully hungry and thirsty and sunburned afore he got himself back to camp.

"I tried to throw him a rope, but I couldn't get it anywhere near to the top o' that cliff. Hopper, he commenced to complain that he was getting sunburned. So I hollered up to him, 'Keep in the shade of a bush, Hopper, and I'll try to figure out a way to get you down again!'

" 'If Hopper can hop up there, I can do it too!' I figgered. 'I'll just have to do like Hopper, and hop back and forth across that stream, carrying just a bit more weight along every hop I hop.'

"It took Hopper a mighty long spell of hopping before he worked himself up to his big jump, but he was stopping betwixt and between every hop to pan out a bit of gold. I figgered that if I just started right in hopping and put stones in my pockets instead of panning out gold nuggets, I could probably jump up and rescue Hopper right quick. Time was awfully important, you see, because the poor fellow wasn't going to be able to stay in that hot sun and hold out for long, what with no water and no food for his *insides,* and not a stitch of clothing for his *out.*

"Wu-a-ll," exclaimed Grampa Herc, "right off, I ate a big meal, so's not to be losing time over food again, and then I began hopping. I'd hop across the stream, put a stone in my pocket, hop back, put another stone in my pocket, back and forth, back and forth," Grampa Herc chanted, beginning to rock back and forth on the lunchroom stool.

All the children and Mr. Gabby and Max, even Uncle Ulysses and the sheriff, began to rock back and forth in time with Grampa Herc's words.

"Stones were getting heavier all the time," Grampa Herc reminded his swaying listeners. "I could feel 'em weighting me down . . . weighting me down . . . just a mite heavier every hop I took . . . back and forth, back and forth. Filled all o' my pants pockets," chanted Grampa Herc. "Shirt pockets too," he added in time to the swaying of his audience. "Put a couple of rocks in my *right boot,* all the time hopping, back and forth . . . *left boot* . . . back and forth. Carried a couple big rocks in my *right hand* . . . in my *left hand.* . . .

"Wu-a-ll!" he shouted, suddenly stopping still, "I quick ripped off all of my clothes, and quick tied a rope around my waist, and quick took another *hop!*"

Everybody's eyes followed Grampa Herc's up, up, up to the ceiling of the lunchroom and focused on a spot near the far corner.

"Whew!" puffed the old man, wiping his brow, and then softly, as though he was still awed and puzzled after all these years, he whispered, *"And there I was, atop the cliff along with Hopper McThud!"*

"You don't say!" said Max.

"Yeah?" asked Mr. Gabby.

"Yup!" said Grampa Herc solemnly. "And we climbed down the rope and packed right up and came back to Ohio."

"What—?" Mr. Gabby started to ask.

"Sure felt sorry for Hopper!" Grampa Herc interrupted, stroking his chin.

"Is that—?" questioned Max.

"In all the excitement," Grampa Herc went on, "he forgot where he'd buried his little bags of gold. He dug that place full o' holes before he gave it up."

"Is that a *true* story?" Max finally managed to ask.

"Often think o' that gold o' Hopper's," answered Grampa Herc. "Think mebbe someday I'll go back west and see if I can find it."

"There's something wrong with that story," grumbled the sheriff, scratching his head, "but hanged if I can figger out what!"

"It would seem a man couldn't hop like that," said Uncle Ulysses. "But I guess he could." He changed his mind quickly, with a glance at Grampa Herc.

"You can't pick that story to pieces!" said Grampa Herc triumphantly.

"It's just like when you roller skate," Homer explained. "After you take off the heavy skates, your feet feel light like feathers, and you keep lifting them higher than natural."

"It's gravity, I expect," Uncle Ulysses elaborated. "Gold and rocks have got gravity pulling them down all the time, just like apples falling off o' trees, and when a man loses all that gravity all of a sudden, he's bound to cut loose with one heck of a hop!"

"Hold everything!" shouted Mr. Gabby with a wild light in his eye. "What an idea!" he raved. "It's better than Vimmy-Swimmys!"

Max seemed to understand what it was all about, and he said, "We could change the box, and we wouldn't have to waterproof them!"

Then Mr. Gabby and Max both started talking at once. "What's the Lonely Ranger got that this old guy hasn't got? Better than Super-Duper! The kids'll go for his line! Let's make him a partner in the firm! Okay? Okay."

"Gramps," said Mr. Gabby, pumping Grampa Herc's hand, "you're a member of the Gabby, Maxwell, and Hercules Container Package and Advertising Company."

"I made a lot of barrels and kegs in my day," reminded Grampa Herc, hearing the words container and package mentioned.

"You don't have to make barrels, Gramps," said Mr. Gabby. "All you gotta do is tell your stories."

"But," cautioned Max, "don't tell them to anybody except partners in the company! We don't want anybody to steal our ideas!"

"What an idea!" raved Mr. Gabby. "C'mon, Max, let's get going!"

"Aren't you goin' to eat your blue-plate specials?" Uncle Ulysses asked with alarm, and he reached quickly to catch up with a bottle of catsup that Max sent rolling along the counter in his enthusiasm.

"We could have singing commercials," Mr. Gabby chuckled, slapping Max on the shoulder.

" 'Merrily we hop along!' " sang Max, to the tune of "Mary Had a Little Lamb," and he and Mr. Gabby went out the door arm in arm, singing, " 'Merrily we hop a-long, hop a-long, hop a-long,' " and roared away in their car.

Uncle Ulysses stood shaking his head over the two untouched blue-plate specials, and the sheriff looked over his glasses and said, "First time I set eyes on that Gabby fellow I thought he ought to be locked up!"

Grampa Hercules apparently still had his mind on his story because he stroked his old chin and said, "You never can tell how gold will affect a fellow!

"Wu-a-ll! Got to get home and feed my chickens," the old man said suddenly. "Nope, no more stories today," he told the children, expertly freeing himself from pleading girls hanging onto sleeves and boys clutching coat tails. He untangled somebody's top string from around his left foot, then promised "some other time," and strode off down the street.

IV. THE GRAVITTY-BITTIES

The following Monday afternoon Homer's mother met him at the door. "Homer, the station agent has just phoned and said that a large express package has arrived for your Grandfather Hercules. Would you please run over and tell him about it?"

"Yup," said Homer.

"And don't stay too long," she reminded quickly, because Homer was already down the steps and almost to the road.

"Where're you going, Homer?" called Freddy from his front porch.

"Grampa Herc has a package at the express office," said Homer, "and I'm on my way over to tell him about it."

"I could come along and help you tell him, Homer," Freddy offered, falling into step beside Homer.

"There he is," said Homer, pointing across the road and up toward the little knoll where Grampa Herc's house and chicken-coops stood.

"You've got a package!" panted Freddy, out of breath from running up the hill.

"At the express office," explained Homer. "The station agent just phoned. Perhaps you'd like to have us come along and see what's in it."

"Wu-a-ll now!" said Grampa Hercules. "Wonder who could be sendin' me an express package? Haven't ordered anything, no birthdays or anniversaries this month. Just let me get my hat and we'll walk down to the station and see what this is all about."

As they crossed the town square the sheriff came out of the barbershop and called, "You've got a package down at the station —came on the afternoon train!"

Grampa Hercules nodded his head and kept right on striding, followed by Homer and Freddy. Ginny Lee and several other girls and boys collected from around the monument and followed, so

60

that by the time Grampa Herc reached the station he had a considerable crowd to help him claim his package. There on the station platform stood a tremendous carton.

"Nothing pasted on it to tell what's inside," Uncle Ulysses stated. "Just says, 'USE NO HOOKS' and 'HANDLE WITH CARE.'"

"Hercules!" called the station agent, pushing through the crowd and handing Grampa Herc a yellow paper. "This telegram just arrived from New York."

Grampa Herc fumbled in his pocket. "Forgot my glasses. Here, Homer, read this for me like a good young un."

Homer read: " 'Have sent you four months' supply of sensational new breakfast food. Stop. Please use as instructed by directions on box. Stop. Anxiously await your experienced reaction before selling product to buying public. Gabby and Maxwell.' "

"Four months' supply of breakfast food!" said Uncle Ulysses with a chuckle.

"That's certainly a lot of food!" said the station agent, starting back to his office.

"*And* a lot of *box tops!*" said Homer.

"Oh, boy!" shouted Freddy. "Let's open the carton and see what they're giving away."

Grampa Hercules took out his pocketknife and carefully slit the tape that sealed the carton. He picked out one of the boxes and read "GRAVITTY-BITTIES" printed in large letters across the front. Then, after squinting a bit, Grampa Herc handed the box to Homer so he could read the fine print.

" 'Gravitty-Bitties,' " read Homer, " 'the breakfast food of champion jumpers. The sensational cereal of packaged power with the *Gravitty Box Bottom.*' "

"What's that?" Ginny Lee asked.

" 'See directions on reverse side,' " Homer read. Then he turned the box over and continued, " 'Eat a box of feather-light Gravitty-Bitties for breakfast every morning for four months and become a champion jumper. All you have to do is this:

" 'First—Eat the Gravitty-Bitties.

" 'Second—Pin the Gravitty-Bitty box bottom, which is made of pure *lead,* to the inside of your coat or jacket. Each Gravitty-Bitty box bottom comes complete with attached safety-catch pin.

" 'And last—Practice jumping.

" '*Be Sure* you eat your box of feather-light enriched Gravitty-Bitties every morning for four months and

" '*Be sure* you pin another pure lead Gravitty-Bitty box bottom inside your jacket every morning for four months. Then, take off your jacket and JUMP! Your friends will be SURPRISED!' "

"I'll be durned," said Uncle Ulysses, scratching his head.

"Don't this setup remind you of a story, Hercules?" asked the sheriff slyly.

"Hercules," called the station agent, "it looks like you're getting to be a popular fellow. Here's another telegram."

"Uh-h? Oh, yes," said Grampa Hercules in a dazed sort of way. He motioned for Homer to read it.

"It says," Homer began, " 'Please time four months' test of Gravitty-Bitty breakfasts to end morning of July Fourth. Stop. Arranging with radio, television, and news services to cover jump. Gabby and Maxwell.' "

"Well, Grampa Hercules," said Uncle Ulysses, "it looks like we'll have a chance to find out what's wrong with that story of yours."

"Now look here!" cried Grampa Hercules. "There's not a thing wrong with that story in its place. These two crazy fellas 're tryin' to put my story in a box and make it something to eat! The trouble

63

with these advertising people is that they don't know where words and stories stop and what *isn't* words and stories begin. They get it all confused and printed on a fancy package and commence to believe it's every word true!"

"Well," said Uncle Ulysses, "in a world full of television and rocket ships, it's sort of hard for anybody not to be confused. I'll admit I'm puzzled," Uncle Ulysses continued. "This theory *sounds* good, but I don't think that *gold* or *rocks* or *Gravitty-Bitty box bottoms* can help a man jump like that. Still, I can't understand why it *wouldn't* work."

"Oh, pshaw!" said the sheriff. "It's just like *all* of Hercules' tales—just like breakin' through the ice, like the clock spull of farrows—I mean *birds*. There's some catch to it, something that's not quite right."

"Now, Sheriff!" began Grampa Hercules.

Ginny Lee put her small hand in Grampa Hercules' wrinkled brown one and said, "Don't you worry about what *he* says. *We* all like your stories!"

"You bet!" said Freddy.

"And," continued Ginny Lee, turning toward the sheriff and Uncle Ulysses, "Grampa Herc will *show* you men on the Fourth of July, so there!"

A loud cheer of approval went up from the crowd of children. Grampa Herc stroked his chin, looking uncomfortable.

Ginny Lee turned to him and inquired anxiously, "Won't you, Grampa Herc?"

"U-u-u-uh-h," mumbled Grampa Hercules in a flustered sort of way, while some of the children cheered and whistled their approval.

"Come on, everybody," Ginny Lee commanded the children. "We'll help Grampa Herc carry his Gravitty-Bitties home."

She supervised most efficiently while each of the children filed by and received several boxes of Gravitty-Bitties. Then Ginny Lee, still hand in hand with Grampa Hercules, led the way, and all the girls and boys carrying heavy lead-bottomed boxes of breakfast food followed behind, leaving the sheriff and Uncle Ulysses standing on the station platform with the large empty carton.

That evening after supper Homer and Freddy sat on a fence, discussing the happenings of the afternoon.

"That will be more exciting than the Fourth of July fireworks, Homer, watching Grampa Herc make his big jump!" said Freddy.

"Ya-ah," said Homer, kicking at a clump of weeds. "I tell you, Freddy, it never fails! Doggonit, you can't trust 'em!"

"But, Homer, don't you think it'll work?" asked Freddy.

"Mebbe," said Homer with a scowl. "It's the sort of thing that nobody can be sure of until it's tried, but did you see the way she looked at him—with her *eyes* I mean! Puts her hand in his and says, 'Won't you, Grampa Herc?' I tell you, Freddy, *you just can't trust girls!*" Ginny Lee managed and bossed and persuaded Grampa Herc into this mess!"

"But, Homer, it's just *got* to work! If you work up to it gradual like, almost anything is possible—like lifting up a bull. I *know* that can be done, I've seen pictures."

"Yeah, that's so," said Homer.

"And like everybody knows," Freddy continued, "right after you take off roller skates your feet sort of hop up off the ground. I sorta suppose if you carried a little bit more, and a little bit more weight every day, why, when you all of a sudden one day *didn't*— why, shucks, Homer, I bet you could almost feel like *flying!*"

"It could be," said Homer hopefully, "and then, too, there's the Gravitty-Bitty stuff."

"Sa-a-a-y, Homer," Freddy interrupted, "did you see that stuff? It's really and truly *feather-light* exactly like it says on the box.

66

You can hardly breathe without blowing it all over the place!"

"Yeah, Freddy, but its being feather-light couldn't help you hop and jump—I don't *think*. But they're *enriched,* and that might help a little bit in hopping and jumping. Vitamins do a lot, you know. I read an article that said vitamins can make a man happy, or well, or brave—all kinds of things, and Mr. Biggs said down at the barbershop that vitamins are supposed to grow hair on bald heads even!"

"Well, see, Homer, it could possibly really and truly work," said Freddy. "Mebbe not work so well as to make a guy jump three hundred feet, but just a hundred feet mebbe, say just to the top of the courthouse steeple, so what are you worried about?"

"Because," said Homer, "if anything should go wrong, Uncle Ulysses and the sheriff would never stop teasing Grampa Herc—and Posty Pratt and the barber and the judge, you know how *they* would laugh. Why, Grampa Herc would never hear the end of it!"

"It would make him mad," Freddy admitted.

"And," said Homer, "it would hurt his feelings! If that ever happens, Grampa Herc would probably retire from storytelling and never tell another!"

"Gosh, Homer, that would be *terrible!*" Freddy agreed. "Perhaps we could persuade him to call the whole thing off."

"It's too late," Homer said sadly. "The men would laugh about his being afraid to try. He should have sent the whole four months' supply of Gravitty-Bitties right back to Mr. Gabby, box bottoms and all."

"We should have told him," said Freddy.

"Shucks," said Homer, "I think Grampa Herc would've thought of it himself if it hadn't been for—" Homer picked up a rock and hurled it at a mailbox. Then both boys walked silently along the side of the road.

"She *is* sort of bossy," Freddy said finally. "But you know, Homer, I think I'd have done the same thing myself if I thought she wanted me to."

"That's what I mean," said Homer, nodding his head grimly. "You can't trust girls! Be seeing you, Freddy." Homer waved, and after hurling one more rock at the mailbox he scuffled off across the yard.

During the next week it became the children's custom to stop by Grampa Hercules' place every day after school to see how he was getting on with his jumping. Although the old man never said as much, everyone thought he seemed just as curious as the next person to see how the experiment would turn out. So curious, in fact, that he started pinning on *four* Gravitty-Bitty box bottoms every morning after breakfast.

"Fourth of July's too long to wait," he said. "This way I'll be all weighted down and rarin' to jump on Saint Patrick's Day!"

Grampa Hercules also had very definite ideas about where to pin on box bottoms, pinning them here and there, on sleeves, suspenders, pants, shirt, and even shoes.

"Distributes the weight better, just like I did with the rocks when I rescued Hopper," he said.

Grampa Hercules did his jumping practice back and forth across the little brook near his place, the one that empties into Curbstone Creek.

Uncle Ulysses stopped by with the sheriff one morning to have a look at Grampa Hercules jumping across the brook.

"You ought to have followed the directions more closely," Uncle Ulysses criticized, "and been more scientific."

"Umpf-f!" grunted Grampa Hercules, taking a hop and straining under the weight of all the lead box bottoms.

"System and science be hanged!" he shouted. Then "Umpf-f!" he grunted and hopped again. "I didn't use that stuff—uhp-f-f! —when I worked up to liftin' bulls—uhmp-f-f!—and horses— uhnpff!" he grunted, taking another jump, "and I'm not gonna

start usin' it now! I declare," he scolded, wiping his brow, "it's a strange world you people're livin' in today. A person can't pick up a pin without peekin' at a statistic. An old storyteller like me can't open his mouth without somebody sayin', 'That ain't accordin' to scientific fact—that ain't been proved!' you say. In the early days people took a man's word for a *few* things, everybody, that is, but a few so-and-so's from Missouri. I'll *prove* it for you!" said Grampa Hercules, and "Hu-m-m-phf!" he hopped again.

Grampa Hercules remained close to home. Homer and Freddy ran errands and tended the chickens, and Ginny Lee and her

friends helped out around the house, because the weight of the pure lead Gravitty-Bitty box bottoms was beginning to have considerable effect on the old man's ability to get about. He kept right at it, though, pinning on four more box bottoms every day and practicing his jumping, rain or shine, without fail.

And the sun always shone. There was no rain, and there was no wind. The month of March (as in the old saying) had come in like a lamb. But on the morning of the day before Saint Patrick's Day, the wind started up with a roar. The rain began pelting down too, and March (as in the old saying) seemed bent on going out like a lion.

Of course everyone in town, when they got up that morning, immediately started hoping for good weather on Saint Patrick's Day for the sake of Grampa Hercules' big jump. With such strong winds and driving rain, everyone kept under cover as much as possible. Children scurried in and out of school and school busses, and citizens like the sheriff and Uncle Ulysses kept close to the stove in the barbershop or in the cozy Ulysses Lunch. Nobody dropped in to see Grampa Hercules during his final day of training.

Saint Patrick's Day morning was bright and clear. Uncle Ulysses' lunchroom was already crowded with interested spectators when Grampa Hercules came in.

"Where're we goin' to run this thing off, Hercules?" asked the sheriff. "Should I stake off an area and block off traffic on the square?"

"Wu-a-ll," said Grampa Hercules, "I hate to disappoint you fellas, but to tell the truth I've already jumped! Yup," he said, "already jumped. You see, I'm an old hand at this kind of thing, and I've known all along that this is the sort of affair that you can't run accordin' to a clock or a schedule. You have to sorta *feel* when the time is right to jump. You know I've been practicing my jumping and hopping down back of my house—hopping back and forth across the brook near where it empties into Curbstone Creek. Well, yesterday evening I was taking a few practice hops, after pinning on the last four box bottoms, when this feeling came on. My coordination was perfect, and I could feel every muscle in my body quivering and surging with power, felt like a race horse clamoring to be off."

"Well, come on and tell us, Hercules," demanded the sheriff impatiently.

Grampa Herc silenced him with a glance and continued, "Yesterday was a bad day, what with the rain and March wind, but I had the feeling that then was the time, so I took a couple more practice hops, then sat down on a log and unpinned all the box bottoms. Yeah, I thought with the weather so bad it wouldn't do for an old fellow like me to go stripping off any of his clothes."

"And *then* you jumped?" asked Uncle Ulysses.

"*Yes indeedy,* I jumped!" said Grampa Herc. "I gave a big spring and took off. Hadn't scarcely got higher than the old sycamore tree before I knew I was in for some real trouble." Grampa Hercules nodded. "Yup, the *wind* caught me and gave me a couple quick turns and then took me right off my course, spinnin' me end over end like a propeller! Of course my hat blew off right away. Had to climb up and fetch it down off the top of the sycamore first thing this morning. Then the wind commenced tugging and pulling at the resta my clothes. I could feel the buttons giving way, one by one. Why, even the laces o' my shoes snapped in that gale of wind—and I can tell you, I was *scared!* I just closed my eyes and hoped for the best! Don't know how long I kept 'em shut, but next thing I remember I opened 'em and found I wasn't moving or twisting any more. I was lying all stretched out in my underwear with straw to all sides of me! I felt myself all over and made for certain that I wasn't hurt, then looked around to find out where I'd lit. Come to find out, I'd come down

74

smack in the middle of a hay stack! Couldn't recognize the barn nearby or any of the surrounding landscape at first glance, but then, after I'd calmed down a mite, it began to dawn on me that I'd been in that neighborhood years before. 'Why, this looks like Top Knot, Indiana,' I thought to myself. 'Hercules, you've missed up on your landmarks. You can't be where you seem to be!' But then I looked out from all the corners of that straw stack, checking the lay of the land, and sure enough, I *was* there!"

"Where?" asked the sheriff.

"Why, I'll tell you where," shouted Grampa Hercules. "I was three and a half miles into the state of Indiana! That wind blew me *nineteen miles* as the crow flies from the spot where I commenced my jump!"

There was a moment's silence, and then Grampa Hercules continued, "Had to wait till it got dark before I could move out of that straw, being dressed only in my underwear. Took me all night, hiking across country and back lanes, to get home by sunup this morning. Caught a bit of cold too, just as I'd expected."

"Now, Hercules!" said the sheriff disdainfully.

"Ha-ah!" snorted Uncle Ulysses.

"You fellas are eying me as though you think I've not told you right about"—Grampa Hercules paused and blew his nose loudly —"you see? I've got a mighty bad cold from tramping nineteen miles in my underwear, and looka here, here's the snag in my hat where it caught atop the old sycamore!" He passed the hat for all to examine.

The sheriff and Uncle Ulysses looked at the hat, then looked at each other and laughed. Then they hurried off toward the barber-shop.

Homer nudged Freddy and whispered, "They're going to spread the news. All the men in town will be laughing at Grampa Herc!"

"Yeah!" whispered Freddy.

"Now what are you young uns whispering about among your-selves?" Grampa Hercules demanded suspiciously. He looked around at the young faces, then abruptly he said, "Good-by," and strode off home.

During the next week the situation proved fully as bad as Homer had expected. Grampa Hercules' feelings were hurt very much indeed. He kept close to his house and chickens on the little knoll. When he did venture out to buy groceries or cough syrup for his cold, the men of the town all laughingly greeted him with embarrassing questions about his big jump.

"Recovered from that championship hop yet, Hercules?" they'd ask.

"Going to make another bi-state jump when the weather improves?"

"Hercules, did I hear that the government was going to give you a contract to carry air mail between here and Kokomo?"

To all these questions Grampa Hercules had little or nothing to say. He went about his business of buying supplies and headed for home as soon as possible. Worst of all, he avoided all the children. He never once walked through the town square and past the monument, and when he saw a group at play he would go out of his way, by walking clear around a block or by taking another street.

"Perhaps when his cold gets better he'll stop by and tell a story," said Ginny Lee.

"I'm afraid," Homer said, "that Grampa Hercules has retired from storytelling and isn't going to tell us any more, *ever!*"

"But, Homer," said Ginny Lee, "that's silly. Why would he *retire?*"

"Because," said Homer, "everybody is laughing and making jokes about his jumping story and his feelings are hurt. He thinks that people the age of Uncle Ulysses and the sheriff, and we children too, are living in a scientific age and don't appreciate anything that's not scientifically proved in laboratories with statistics and theories."

"But that's silly!" Ginny Lee repeated. "We'll have to do something about that!"

"Yeah!" Homer said disdainfully. "*You* helped boss him into this mess, so let's *you* help get him out of it!"

"Homer Price!" Ginny Lee said indignantly. "You know very well that you and Freddy and all the other girls and boys were just as curious as I was! You *all* wanted to see him make a championship jump. I think it's terrible of the men to laugh about Grampa Hercules losing his clothes in the wind!"

"Sure," said Freddy, "but what can we do about it?"

"We *girls* will do something about it!" said Ginny Lee firmly. "Come," she commanded all the jacks players. "I have a cousin who is a Girl Scout in Top Knot, Indiana. We'll write her a letter and have her send Grampa Herc's clothes back."

She turned on her heel and, nose in air, started to lead the girls away on their errand.

"She'll never find them!" Homer taunted.

"Yes, she will too," said Ginny Lee, "with the whole troop to help her and the Brownies too—why, they'll look in every straw stack in the county. Mu-u-umf!" she finished, with an appropriate expression and stiffly walked away, leaving Freddy and Homer by themselves.

"If they find them," said Freddy, "then Grampa Herc could really prove how far he'd jumped."

"Yeah," said Homer, and he sat there quietly for a minute or two, watching a robin hunt worms. Then finally he said casually, "You know the brook where Grampa Herc practiced his jumping?"

"Yeah," answered Freddy, "I've been fishing there hundreds of times. It's not very wide."

"But it's deep," said Homer, and both boys sat silent for a moment.

"The grass and mud along the banks get sort of slick and slippery in the rain," said Homer, looking at Freddy out of the corner of his eye.

"I know," said Freddy. "I hooked a big one right near there one time and the bank was so slippery I almost went in. He got away," Freddy continued dreamily. "He got away, hook, line, and sin-sinker!"

Freddy sat up with a start.

"Yup! Lots of 'em!" said Homer, getting to his feet. "Let's go fishing, Freddy."

"You bet," said Freddy with a grin, "and in case we don't catch any fish we could go swimming and catch cold!"

"Now listen, Freddy, I've got a plan," said Homer as they started off. "The only trouble is, we gotta get Ginny Lee and her friends in the Top Knot troop of Girl Scouts to help out. Now we'll . . ."

A few days later almost every child in Centerburg was in the town square and playing busily with jacks or tops or at some game or other.

After the afternoon train had come in, Homer gave his top one last spin and walked across to the post office. He walked in and sort of became busy with a scratchy pen at the writing desk, while he watched Posty Pratt sort out the afternoon mail. Posty finished sorting out the cards and letters, then started on the packages.

"Dum-duum-de-dum," hummed Posty while he worked. Then he looked up and called to Homer, "Here's a parcel-post package for your Grandfather Hercules."

"I'll tell him," offered Homer, tossing down the pen and dashing out the door. He walked across to the monument and announced in a loud voice, "Grampa Herc has a package at the post office."

Without saying a word, the persuasive and usually talkative Ginny Lee started off in the direction of Grampa Hercules' house.

"Better wait about five minutes," Homer whispered to Freddy. "She might need a little time to persuade him."

At the end of that time Freddy sauntered over to the barbershop and Homer toward the lunchroom.

Besides a few citizens collecting their mail, the post office seemed unusually crowded with children. Posty Pratt was being his usual grouchy self, and when Uncle Ulysses "just happened" to drop in with Homer, and the sheriff "just happened" to drop in with Freddy, Posty grouchingly answered their questions.

"No!" he grumbled. " 'Tain't from New York. No return address on it, but it's postmarked—let me see now," said Posty, holding Grampa Hercules' package to the light, "it's postmarked *Top Knot,* Indiana."

"I *beg* your pardon!" commanded Ginny Lee, pushing her way through the group and holding tight to Grampa Hercules' hand as though she were afraid he might suddenly decide to run away.

Grampa Hercules silently signed the receipt for his package and turned to go, trying all the while to pretend he didn't know there was anyone else within miles of the post office.

"Aren't you going to open it now?" asked Ginny Lee sweetly, looking up at Grandpa Hercules.

The old man hesitated, and Uncle Ulysses quickly whipped out his pocketknife. "Here's a knife to cut the string. Here, let me do it for you."

Then, after a few seconds of crinkling of brown wrapping paper, there was a loud thump as a pair of stringless old shoes hit the floor. Then *all* of Grampa Hercules' clothes came tumbling out of the paper package. The old man pawed them over for some seconds, then he grinned and held up the jacket for all to see.

"Tsk, tsk!" he said, smiling. "Now would you just look here, how the wind took those buttons off, as neat as if it had been done with a scissors." He looked closely at all the children's faces and Ginny Lee blushed.

"Now look at my *wallet!*" exclaimed Grampa Hercules. "I'd heard tell of this and seen it in pictures how tornadoes could drive a straw clean through a piece of wood, but this beats all!" he said. "This straw sticking right through a hole in the leather, made as round and clean as if it had been done with a hammer and nail!"

Freddy smiled and fidgeted a bit while Grampa Hercules' long arms grabbed the wrapping paper from Uncle Ulysses and the sheriff, who were checking the postmark, Top Knot, Indiana, that was stamped there.

"No return address!" remarked Grampa Hercules, looking the wrapper over carefully, "so I'll never know who to thank. But wasn't it a nice idea for somebody to look in my wallet and find out who I was, and send me my clothes—a very nice idea!" said Grampa Herc, looking around.

Homer studied the expressions on Uncle Ulysses' and the sheriff's faces and managed not to blush—very much.

"Posty!" demanded Grampa Hercules, slapping a coin down on the counter. "Sell me one of those important-looking big stamped envelopes. I have to write those two advertising rascals in New York and tell 'em their Gravitty-Bitties are too danged dangerous to sell to the public!"

"Mebbe," said Homer casually, "Gravitty-Bitty jumping would be possible if they printed a few precautions in the directions on the box—like 'Don't Jump in Bad Weather' and 'Allow for Prevailing Winds.' "

"Oh, that *jumping* part, that's *nothing*. But you know, those fellas are thinking of trying to get folks to *eat* that stuff! Yep, those fellas just couldn't keep from overdoing it with that 'feather-light enriched' business."

"Did the Gravitty-Bitties give you indigestion?" asked Ginny Lee solicitously.

"Me eat that stuff?" Grampa Hercules asked, and "Pfuftht!" he spat at one of the post-office receptacles. "I fed it to the chickens, and a mighty good thing too!" he said emphatically. "But those chickens haven't been the same since! The trouble started about four or five days after they began eatin' Gravitty-Bitties. I was gathering eggs, just like always, when by accident I happened to drop an egg—and this egg didn't *break*. I didn't think a thing of it at the time, didn't suspect a thing, you see, and the egg sorta settled down on the cement floor and I reached down and grabbed it quick, before it could blow away. Looking back, I can't see for the life of me why I didn't have sense enough to stop feeding those hens Gravitty-Bitties.

"Wu-a-ll!" exclaimed Grampa Hercules, "a few days later I started out at the regular time to collect eggs. Would you believe it?—there wasn't a single egg in any o' the nests! 'Some animal or person is raiding my henhouse,' I thought to myself, so I set a

83

few traps and put a padlock on the door. Next day and day after, the same thing happened, no traps sprung, the lock not tampered with, and *not a single solitary egg* in any o' the nests.

"I was plumb completely puzzled, and I decided to keep my eyes and ears open. Next morning I could hear the hens clucking and carrying on as if they'd just laid a mess of eggs, and I dropped everything and rushed into the henhouse. Got there in time to find a couple o' hens cut-cut-ca-dud-dutting as though they'd right that minute moved off their nests after layin' some eggs.

" 'Got here on time this time!' I complimented myself and reached down into the nests to gather the eggs. I felt around and I looked. I put on my glasses and looked some more, and nope! not a single solitary egg. Those two hens and me stood there dumfounded, staring down into the nests. They were just as puzzled as me, you see. You can't fool a hen about such things. *They* know better than anybody when they've just laid an egg. I tell you, I was at my wits' end to know what could be whisking those eggs out of the nest the second the hens unset themselves. It made me howling, swearing mad. 'Oh, you!' I yelled. 'You double-enriched vanilla-colored unprintable something-or-other that's stealin' my eggs!' I raised my eyes—and *there* was the answer.

"Wu-a-ll, do you know, those eggs were falling right straight *up* and breaking on the ceiling? Yup. Those hens had been eating feather-light enriched Gravitty-Bitties, and it was playing hob with egg production! The eggs didn't have a mite o' gravity to

84

'em, and the minute a hen moved off a nest after laying an egg, that egg would fall right spang up to the ceiling and smash among the rafters! The waste of it all was appalling," said Grampa Herc, stroking his chin.

"Couldn't you scramble some of them for breakfast?" asked Homer. "That's a good way to use up broken eggs."

"Thought of that," said Grampa Herc, moving toward the door. "But I had to turn the frying pan upside down to keep 'em from falling up to the ceiling o' the kitchen. A complete waste— that's what it was. I had to scrape 'em off the henhouse ceiling and ease them out the window and watch the shells and yolks go floatin' away. Things are getting back to normal again now," Grampa Herc said. "Every morning I have to scrape one or two down, but now most o' the eggs are heavy enough to stay put in a basket. And speakin' of baskets—that reminds me of a story. But come on, all you young uns, let's get out of this stuffy post office and over to the monument steps."

Grampa Hercules, followed by all of his young admirers, surged happily out of the post office. The old man, with a gay twinkle in his eye, called back over his shoulder, "Hey, Sheriff— you too, Ulysses—if you're not busy tomorrow morning along about egg gatherin' time, come on out and I'll scrape down a couple of eggs for you!"

The sheriff and Uncle Ulysses didn't say a word, but that's not surprising, because Grampa Hercules had the last words to say in *this* story. He said 'em too, didn't he?

85

EXPERIMENT 13

EXPERIMENT 13

THE CENTERBURG courthouse clock was just striking eight as Homer rode into the town square. He parked his bike in front of the barbershop, poked his finger into a crack in the wooden barberpole, and pulled out a key. After unlocking the door and putting up the shades, Homer swept the floor.

By quarter of nine Homer had finished with all of his opening-up chores. He started looking through the stack of old magazines, the same magazines that had been there last Saturday and the Saturday before, the same magazines that had been in the barbershop since Homer started working there. Homer had looked at them all a hundred times, so he just sat looking out of the window, waiting for the barber to arrive at nine o'clock.

Through the barbershop window he watched the sheriff walk across the square at ten minutes to nine, as usual, and go into Uncle Ulysses' lunchroom for breakfast.

He watched the mayor drive up and go into the town hall at five minutes of nine, as usual.

The courthouse clock struck nine, and Homer yawned. Just for variety he looked in the mirror, so that he could see the town square backwards. Then, by sitting in the barber chair and leaning way back, he looked in the mirror and saw the town square *upside down* and backwards. Homer smiled as he watched the barber come out of the lunchroom upside down.

Boosting himself out of the barber chair, Homer looked at the clock and thought, "He's a little bit late, as usual!" Then he said, "Gosh!" to nobody in particular. "Everything is so *usual* around here. Seems as though nothing ever happens here any more."

"Morning, Homer," the barber said as he came in. "I see we are open and ready for business." It was the same thing that the barber said every Saturday morning.

"Good morning, Mr. Biggs," said Homer, watching the barber take off his coat and hat and hang them on the same hook he always hung them on.

"Now he will put on his eyeshade," thought Homer, "and his white jacket with the two buttons missing. Next he will take his razor from the little white cabinet marked sterilizer and begin to strop it."

While the barber was stropping his razor the door opened and Homer knew exactly who it would be. He said, "Hello, Sheriff!" without even having to look.

"Good morning, everybody," the sheriff greeted and sat down in the barber chair to be shaved.

Just as the barber finished shaving the sheriff and Homer finished shining the sheriff's shoes, Uncle Ulysses arrived right on schedule and just as usual.

"Anything new?" asked Uncle Ulysses.

Homer shook his head, and the barber said, "Nope."

"Things are mighty slow," said the sheriff with a yawn.

"No new magazines?" asked Uncle Ulysses hopefully, looking through the same old stack. Then he glanced up and said, "Uh-owh!" and the sheriff, the barber, Homer, and Uncle Ulysses moved over to the window to look.

Dulcy Dooner and Lawyer Stobbs were hurrying across the square just as fast as they could go.

"Something's up!" said the barber.

"Where are they going?" mused Uncle Ulysses.

"Looks like they're beaded for the hank—I mean headed for the bank!" said the sheriff.

"The bank doesn't open until nine-thirty," said Homer.

Clear across the square they heard Dulcy bang on the door of the bank and shout, "Open up! Open the door, I say!" And they saw the door of the bank open two minutes before nine-thirty and Dulcy and Lawyer Stobbs go inside.

"First time the bank ever let anybody in before nine-thirty for as long as I remember," said Uncle Ulysses.

"Dulcy is sure excited about something," said the sheriff. "Usually he isn't even up this time of day."

"Say, Homer," said the barber, looking in the cash drawer, "I seem to be running out of change. You take these two dollars and run over to the bank and get me some nickels."

"All right, Mr. Biggs," Homer agreed, and the sheriff and the barber and Uncle Ulysses stood by the open door while he ran across the square and into the bank.

"Sh-h, listen!" said Uncle Ulysses. "I can hear Dulcy shoutin'."

"He just yelled 'ninety grand,'" whispered the barber.

"No, he didn't," Uncle Ulysses disagreed. "He said 'I demand.'"

"Here comes Homer," said the sheriff. "We'll soon know what the fuss is all about. What's goin' on, son?" he asked.

"Has Dulcy got ninety grand?" asked the barber, reaching for his two dollars' worth of nickels.

"What's he demanding?" asked Uncle Ulysses.

"Dulcy is demanding and *maybe* he's got ninety grand. That's what he's demanding to find out," said Homer. "Dulcy's uncle Durpee Dooner died of fever over in Africa and he left everything to Dulcy."

"That's nothing to be so mad about," said Uncle Ulysses.

"Naw," the barber agreed, "Dulcy will be a rich man."

"Havin' money should make him easier to get along with," said the sheriff.

"Well, Dulcy hasn't got any money, not yet anyway," said Homer. "All he's got so far is that old greenhouse and ten acres of land where Durpee Dooner used to run his seed business before he got to be so famous."

"Why, Durpee Dooner must have made lots of money," said the barber.

"Sure!" agreed the sheriff. "Bein' such a samous fientist—I mean famous scientist—and goin' on expeditions all over the world!"

"Well, Dulcy and Lawyer Stobbs can't find any money. They have looked everywhere and gone through all of the papers. There were no bank books, or stocks, or bonds, or anything. All they found was a key to a safe deposit box, and that must be where all the money is. Dulcy is so mad because they are making him sign a lot of papers before they let him go in the vault and unlock the box."

"It sounds like things have calmed down over there," said Uncle Ulysses, cocking an ear. "I think I'll just walk across and cash a small check."

"I been needin' a new blotter, so I'll just come along," said the sheriff.

The barber went along to get some more change, and Homer ran along behind to take the sheriff his coat. No telling, the sheriff might need his badge.

As they went into the bank the banker was just opening the heavy door of the vault.

"Just step inside, Mr. Dooner," he said. "Here is the deposit box, number one hundred and thirteen."

"It's about time," growled Dulcy, jabbing his key into the lock.

The sheriff, the barber, Uncle Ulysses, and Homer all crowded up to the counter and peered through the bars to watch.

Dulcy turned the key and pulled out the box. His hands shook so much with excitement that he had trouble opening the lid. He managed to get it open and then he let out a wild howl!

"What kinda joke is this?" he yelled, and he jumped around

something awful, banging the vault, bumping the banker, and bumping the lawyer.

"Take care, Mr. Dooner! You'll break it!" shouted the banker, grabbing Dulcy by the arm before he could throw the something that was in the box.

"Calm down, Dulcy," the lawyer demanded. "Let's be sensible and take it out in the light and examine it."

"Of all the lousy tricks!" growled Dulcy, holding a small glass jar up to the light.

"What's in it?" Uncle Ulysses demanded through the paying teller window.

"Aw, nuts!" said Dulcy, giving the jar a shake.

"Did you say nuts?" asked the sheriff.

"No!" yelled Dulcy. "It's a lousy jar of *seeds!*"

"A most unusual place for keeping seeds," said the banker.

"Maybe they are unusual seeds," Homer suggested.

"Yes, Dulcy, they are no doubt very valuable seeds," said the lawyer. "That little glass jar might be worth a fortune. Why else would Durpee Dooner keep it locked up in the bank? Look here, there's a label that says *Experiment 13*."

The thought of owning a jar of valuable seeds made Dulcy less mad, but he was far from happy. He shook his head sadly and said, "People inherit money every day, and I have to be the one that inherits a jar of seeds—an experiment at that!"

"What are you going to do with your seeds, Dulcy?" asked Homer.

"Well," said Dulcy, rubbing his chin and frowning at the jar, "I'll plant some of them, I guess." He crammed the jar of seeds into his pocket and started for the door.

"Just a minute, Dulcy," the lawyer cautioned. "Better keep them locked up here in the bank and take out some of them when you are ready to plant."

"Yes, by all means, Mr. Dooner," advised the banker. "The seeds are apparently very valuable, and you must protect them."

Dulcy thought for a minute and then did as the lawyer and the banker suggested. He locked the jar of seeds up in the deposit box and went off to his greenhouse to prepare a place to plant.

"Too bad Dulcy didn't find a nice stack of government savings bonds in the deposit box," said Uncle Ulysses when they had arrived back at the barbershop.

"Yup!" said the sheriff. "With savings bonds you know just what's what."

"Dulcy's Uncle Durpee was a great scientist," reminded the barber, "and that jar of seeds might be worth millions."

"Durpee was a great hand at breeding new plants and improving old ones," said Uncle Ulysses. "He was an up-and-coming fellow for his generation—far ahead of his time."

"Remember the giant squash he developed?" asked the barber.

"Yup," said the sheriff, "and remember the Durpee Tremadous Tomentoes—I mean Tremendous Tomatoes?"

"The Strawberry Tree was the best thing, I always thought," said Homer.

"But the Durpee Dooner Honey Onion was the most remarkable plant he ever bred," Uncle Ulysses asserted. "Looked just like any old onion but tasted just like honey. A Honey Onion pie with meringue on top is one of the world's best foods. Durpee Dooner was a genius, no doubt about it!"

"Well, what do you think Dulcy's seeds will grow into?" asked the barber.

"They were little bitsy things like grass seed," said Homer.

"Something rare that old Durpee brought back from one of his expeditions to Asia or Africa, no doubt," said Uncle Ulysses.

"No," said Homer, "the jar was labeled *Experiment 13,* so the seeds must be for some sort of plants that he developed himself."

"Farmer's Almanac says a mild spring," said the sheriff.

"Time to start planting next month," said the barber.

"It'll still be a long time though before we find out what Dulcy's seeds grow into," said the sheriff.

"Dulcy's got a greenhouse," reminded Uncle Ulysses.

"Golly," said Homer, "Dulcy can plant *today!"*

And Dulcy did plant that same day. By eleven o'clock he was back downtown with a truck, buying fertilizer and vitamin plant food. And he was back at the bank again before noon to get some seeds. He carefully counted out twelve seeds, and one more for good measure, into an envelope. Once more he locked up the glass jar in his safe deposit box and rushed off in the direction of his greenhouse.

By four o'clock, when Homer stopped by the greenhouse, there was Dulcy inside admiring the thirteen damp mounds of earth where he had planted his seeds.

"Hello, Mr. Dooner," said Homer.

"Hello, Homer," said Dulcy. "I'm pretty tired, and my back is sore from haulin' fertilizer and from spadin'."

"You need some help," Homer suggested. "School is out next month, and Freddy and I could help out doing hoeing and spraying—that is, if the seeds grow into anything."

"You're hired, Homer, and Freddy too!" said Dulcy. "They'll grow all right," he added confidently. "I put two bushels of vitamin plant food around each seed."

"Whe-e-ew!" whistled Homer. "What kind of plants do you think they will be, Dulcy?"

"I dunno," said Dulcy. "But whatever they are, they'll be the biggest and the best."

Sunday afternoon Homer called Freddy on the phone and said, "Hi, Freddy. Have you heard about Dulcy's seeds?"

"Gosh, yes, Homer! Everybody in Centerburg's heard about Dulcy's seeds," said Freddy. "Everybody's talking about them. The minister even preached about them this morning. *'If that's what you sow, that's what you reap.'* "

"Dulcy's already planted thirteen of them," said Homer.

"Yeah, I know," Freddy said. "And the jar said *Experiment 13*. My grandmother says no good can come of that."

"That's just superstition," said Homer. "You're not superstitious, are you, Freddy? Because Dulcy's going to give us a job

watering, weeding and taking care of the plants when school's out."

"Oh, gosh, Homer, that'll be swell. Mebbe they will be Strawberry Trees!"

"Nobody knows," said Homer. "But working for Dulcy we'll find out as soon as anybody. We'll stop at Dulcy's tomorrow after school and see what's happening."

"Okay, Homer," said Freddy. "Good-by."

"Good-by, Freddy," said Homer. "See you tomorrow."

Homer and Freddy stopped at the greenhouse the next day after school; they stopped every day all week, and nothing exciting was going on. The seeds had not come up. Dulcy was getting more and more restless and complaining about his back. Along about Friday he started complaining about a stiff neck from watching so steadily for the seeds to come up.

On Saturday morning Homer was late getting to the barbershop. He rushed in and shouted, "They're up!"

"What's up, son?" asked the sheriff.

"Dulcy's plants! Dulcy's plants are up, all thirteen of them!" Homer said.

"Let's go look!" said Uncle Ulysses, throwing down his magazine.

And the barber and Homer and Uncle Ulysses went over to the greenhouse with the sheriff in his car.

"Look!" said Dulcy, proudly displaying the thirteen tender green shoots.

"Healthy-looking plants," said the barber.

"You can almost see them grow!" said Uncle Ulysses.

"You *can* see them grow, if you look closely," said Dulcy, and he started scooping vitamin plant food out of a bag and sprinkling it generously around the plants.

Even with a truckload of vitamin plant food to help out, the plants took weeks to get as high as Homer's head. The tallest one of the thirteen plants came just to the bottom of his ear on the day school was out and Homer and Freddy started working at the greenhouse.

They sprinkled the plants with vitamin plant food and they sprinkled them with water. They carried bags of fertilizer and they listened to Dulcy complain about his back.

"Gosh, Homer, it seems like it takes forever for a plant to grow anything but stems and leaves," Freddy complained. "Why can't these things make a few berries or squashes or something, so we'll know what they are?"

"They have got a lot of stems and leaves," Homer agreed. "Sometimes when I look at them I think they'll be bushes, and other times they remind me of vines."

"They're growing faster now that the weather is warmer," said Freddy. "Look, Homer, this one has grown almost a foot today!"

Sure enough, when Homer stood next to the plant the top reached way above his ear; it was way above his *head*.

The next morning when Homer and Freddy arrived at Dulcy's the tops of the plants were right up touching the glass roof of the greenhouse.

"We have to break out some sections of the roof and give them room to grow," shouted Dulcy.

"Gosh, Dulcy, they're going to be trees!" Freddy exclaimed.

"They're really a-growin' now, son!" said Dulcy with a happy chuckle. "You boys grab a couple of hammers and start knockin' some openings in the roof. You want to be careful," he cautioned, "when you break the glass, that it doesn't hurt the plants."

While Dulcy went off downtown to get another truckload of vitamin plant food, Homer and Freddy climbed around on the roof knocking out openings for the plants to grow through.

Freddy swung his hammer, and a pane of glass went out with a loud crash! and a few small pieces slid tinkle-tinkle down the slant of the roof.

"This is the most fun we've had on this job yet, Freddy," shouted Homer with a laugh.

"Yeah, Homer, but there will be a lot of"—*crash*-tinkle-tinkle—"pieces to pick up," said Freddy as he swung his hammer down.

"That's the sort of job that hurts Dulcy's back," said Homer, stopping to rest. "Holy smoke, Freddy! Look at 'em grow!"

"Wow!" said Freddy, and he dropped his hammer.

The plants were pushing right up through the holes in the glass. It seemed as though they were glad to be out in the warm summer sunshine. Homer peered through the glass and saw a large stalk pushing against the roof. He bashed out a hole and the plant popped through, spread its leaves, and seemed so grateful that Homer politely said, "You're welcome," without thinking.

By the time Dulcy returned with the vitamin plant food every single stalk was through the roof, pushing its way into the sunshine, the new green leaves rustling in the summer breeze. Dulcy went right to work, spreading vitamin plant food around the bases of the stalks, while Homer and Freddy picked up the glass.

As stories of how Dulcy's plants were growing spread through Centerburg, people began to come out to have a look. Dulcy charged fifty cents admission to the greenhouse and made

fifty-nine dollars the first afternoon. By the end of the week, however, business was bad. Not that the plants stopped growing, or that people stopped coming out to look. The plants grew faster than ever—that was the trouble. There was three times as much plant *outside* as there was *inside* the greenhouse. Large crowds gathered on the road every day to watch them grow. Dulcy reduced the price of admission to ten cents but still not many came inside. He was pretty mad about it, but there was not a thing he could do.

"After all, you can't keep people from lookin' at a forest in the middle of a ten-acre lot," said Uncle Ulysses, and that's just about what Dulcy's plants looked like.

One day the rumor went around that there were melons eight feet across inside the greenhouse. Business improved, but not for long, because there were no melons, not even little ones. There were no berries or fruit of any kind, no vegetables, not even a suggestion of a blossom.

"They ain't very pretty plants," said the sheriff, who was on hand every day to handle the traffic problem.

"They're pretty enough," said Dulcy, taking offense, "and bigger than anything you will ever grow!"

"The plants have a familiar shape," said Homer, "and it seems as though I ought to recognize the leaves."

"Maybe they're potatoes, and under the ground," Freddy suggested.

"If they're potatoes, Dulcy," said the sheriff with a chuckle, "you'll have to find a sheam stovel—I mean steam shovel—to dig 'em out."

"Just you wait and see!" Dulcy shouted. "These plants will grow the biggest—the biggest—well, the biggest *somethings* ever grown," and he stamped into his greenhouse to spread on more vitamin plant food.

Two whole weeks went by and Dulcy's plants were producing nothing more remarkable than leaves and stems, but leaves and stems they produced like mad. The plants had become the most important feature of the Centerburg skyline, towering way above the Centerburg courthouse and the smokestack of the Enders Products Company.

"I don't think they're going to bear anything," the barber said one day at lunch in Uncle Ulysses' lunchroom. "They're using up all their strength putting out shoots and leaves. Dulcy should have pruned them down."

"It'll be a big disappointment to Dulcy," said Uncle Ulysses. "He's worked harder on those plants of his than he has since he put up the street signs out at Enders Heights."

"He can try again next year and keep 'em pruned," said the sheriff, brushing a doughnut crumb from his mustache. "He's got plenty more seeds locked up in the bank."

The door opened and, in no special hurry, Homer walked in and sat down at the counter.

"Hello, Homer," said Uncle Ulysses. "Have a doughnut, fresh from the machine."

"No, thank you, Uncle Ulysses," Homer replied, and he sat quietly at the counter, watching the automatic doughnut machine make doughnuts.

"You not feeling well?" Uncle Ulysses inquired.

"I'm feeling all right," Homer replied. Then he announced, "I know what Dulcy's plants are."

"You do?" asked Uncle Ulysses, and everyone rushed to the lunchroom window and looked across the square to where Dulcy's plants rose high above the trees and buildings on the far side.

"You can just make out from here," said Homer. "There are thousands and thousands of buds on top."

"They look familiar," said the barber.

"That's what I've thought for weeks," said Homer. "It's the size that fools you. Hold your hand so as to cover the trees and buildings and pretend for a minute that the plants are ordinary size."

Everybody did as Homer suggested; then one of the customers began to giggle, then another, and finally all the people in the lunchroom began to laugh.

"Poor Dulcy!" laughed the barber, holding his sides.

"He'll never get over this," chuckled Uncle Ulysses. "The town will never stop teasing him. Dulcy's plants are just giant-size *weeds!*"

"Yes, but what kind of weeds?" Homer asked without laughing. Everybody looked again. This time nobody laughed.

"Jiminy Zeus!" cried Uncle Ulysses.

The barber gulped and said, "I'll have to leave town!"

"So will I!" said another customer.

"Me too, I'm leaving today!" said another.

"Dad gum!" the sheriff said. "Now who'd ever thought them plants was *wagreed!*"

"They're ragweed, all right," said Homer, "and I expect they'll blossom in a few days."

"We'd better get the mayor and go see Dulcy," Uncle Ulysses suggested, and the sober little group from the lunchroom started for the town hall. The dentist and several patients came out to see what was going on, and they joined the group. So did the plumber, the jeweler, the printer, and the druggist.

"I have a feeling," said the barber, taking leave of the gathering crowd, "that Dulcy will be in one of his arguing moods. I'm going right home and pack my bag. Just the thought of those things makes me sne-sn-s-*hahuruschooh!*—sneeze."

"An awful lot of folk are troubled with hay fever," said the druggist. "Reminds me I had better order a carload of paper handkerchiefs."

"When all those thousands of buds open up and start filling the air with pollen, this place is going to look like the dust bowl," said the dentist.

Uncle Ulysses and the sheriff went on into the mayor's office, while the others waited outside.

Almost at once the mayor came rushing out of the town hall. He shaded his eyes with his hand, looked solemnly up and across the square at Dulcy's thirteen colossal ragweeds silhouetted against the afternoon sky.

Everybody knew that the mayor was susceptible to hay fever, so they were not at all surprised when he pulled out his handkerchief, just from force of habit. For a minute it looked as if the mayor might start running; but he tucked away his handkerchief, squared his shoulders, and started walking grimly toward Dulcy's.

The crowd followed along behind.

Dulcy came running out to meet them. "They're budding!" he shouted. "They got thousands and thousands of buds! Howdy, Mayor," he greeted. "I was just about to come see you. I wanted to ask you, would you please send the Fire Department out here so's I can cut off a few sprigs of buds to exhibit? My ladder is too small to reach to the lowest branches."

The mayor was slightly taken aback by Dulcy's request and couldn't think of what to say or how to begin.

"I could cut off a few sprigs for you, Mayor," said Dulcy generously, to help the mayor decide. "They'll look mighty nice in a vase in your office when the blossoms come out."

"Dulcy, I—I—" the mayor began and could not continue.

Dulcy Dooner looked around at the solemn faces of the crowd. "What's the matter? This is a big thing for Centerburg! Don't you frown at me, Sheriff, I'm bein' a good citizen. My plants will put this town on the map. I'm doin' a lot for this town, so how about loanin' me the town hook and ladder?"

"Dulcy, I—ah—we—" began the mayor unhappily. "As

mayor of Centerburg, I am sorry to inform you that your plants are *ragweeds*."

Dulcy swallowed hard and craned his neck to look up at his tremendous weeds. In the unhappy silence the gay singing of the birds seemed out of place, and the slight rustle of the giant ragweed leaves suddenly sounded ominous in the summer afternoon.

"Ragweeds? Why, durned if they ain't!" said Dulcy. He seemed disappointed that there would be no fruit or berries to sell, but then he smiled and said, "Well, anyway, I got the biggest dang ragweeds in the world! That'll make Centerburg famous! So look, Mayor, how about the ladder?" he asked.

"See here, Dulcy," said the mayor, "ragweed pollen gives people hay fever!"

Dulcy looked around at the worried faces. "Shucks! Don't you trouble yourselves about me. I'll be all right. I never get hay fever."

"In the interest of public health and pursuit of happiness, for the best interest of the town of Centerburg, I ask you as a good citizen to cut down your ragweeds," said the mayor.

"Cut 'em down?" cried Dulcy. "Cut my ragweeds?" he asked as though he could not believe his ears. "No!" he shouted. "No, I won't cut 'em down." And the citizens watched Dulcy turn on his heel, stamp into his greenhouse, and slam the door.

"Didn't argue much," said the sheriff tartly.

The mayor glanced uneasily up at the thousands of giant ragweed buds swaying innocently in the breeze.

"Sword of Damocles!" Uncle Ulysses exclaimed softly. "In a matter of hours the buds will open, the pollen will—I hate to think of it!"

"Time is important," said the mayor. "We must hold a special town meeting this very evening and decide what to do. Everyone come to the town hall at seven-thirty. Until then, I'll be at my desk, and I will welcome any and all suggestions," he added humbly, "of how to deal with this, the greatest and gravest threat our town has ever known."

"Homer," Freddy said on the way back to town, "my grandmother was right—*Experiment 13,* thirteen plants."

"Superstitious!" Homer replied. "Let's go along with Uncle Ulysses and see what's going to happen."

Uncle Ulysses, the sheriff, the dentist, the printer, Homer, and Freddy found the barber, suitcase in hand, tucking the key to his shop into the crack in the barberpole. They persuaded him to wait over and attend the town meeting that evening, so he opened his shop and invited them all in.

"If ordinary ragweed gives some people hay fever," the printer reasoned, "then these things will be enough to affect everybody!"

"This town will sneeze itself plumb out of the state of Ohio!" the sheriff declared.

"They're growing just west of town too," the dentist said. "The prevailing winds will blow all the pollen smack down our throats."

"Ulysses, you're a man of ideas," said the barber. "What are we going to do?"

Uncle Ulysses was thinking hard. He paced the floor and said, "We could air-condition the town, but it would cost a lot. Not enough time either. Then again, we might drop dry ice in the clouds from an airplane and make it rain. That would keep down the pollen."

"What clouds?" the barber asked gloomily, looking out at the clear blue sky.

"Dulcy might change his mind," said the printer.

"Not Dulcy," said the sheriff. "We might as well decide to take what's comin' and all go to bed with a big supply of haper pand-kerchiefs—I mean perper kerpanchiefs—chaper handkepips—dad gum! You know what I mean—tensing clissues!"

Nobody knew what to do. There was a long line of people waiting to buy tickets at the railroad station. Just like the barber, other businessmen, the plumber, the hardware dealer, the jeweler, even Lawyer Stobbs, were closing their shops and offices and hanging out cards saying:

OUT OF TOWN
REOPENING
SHORTLY AFTER
THE FIRST FROST

But everybody stayed in town to attend the town meeting as a last hope.

Toward seven o'clock Centerburg was a town of gloom. As the sun dropped lower in the sky, groups of residents gathered in the square, and as the sun dropped lower the shadows lengthened.

The longest shadow by far was the shadow of Dulcy's thirteen giant ragweeds; and the people watched them extend across and darken the square and ease slowly up and darken Uncle Ulysses' lunchroom, up and darken the movie theater, and last of all the steeple of the Methodist church.

From one corner of the square there came angry shouts, "Let s chop 'em down! Burn 'em! Spray 'em with weed killer! Spray Dulcy too!"

But the sheriff was right on the job. "Hold on, boys!" he shouted. "You can't destroy private property in this town. Let's get on into the meeting and solve this thing regular!" And he headed the disturbers into the town hall along with everybody else.

Everybody was there, yes, everybody. Dulcy came too. He walked into the hall at the very last minute, and all eyes were turned to the rear where Dulcy stood with the people who could not find seats.

Seeing that his fellow citizens expected him to say something, Dulcy cleared his throat and said, "I been thinkin'. We could solve this problem the democratic way just as easy as that!" He snapped his fingers, and a murmur of hope sounded through the hall.

"Yeah," said Dulcy, gathering courage, "Centerburg doesn't need no crop o' ragweed!"

At this the murmur grew louder, and someone shouted, "Good boy, Dulcy!"

"This town doesn't need ragweeds," he repeated. Then he took a deep breath and said, "When the government decides the country doesn't need cotton, the government pays the farmer to plow it under. When the government decides there's too many potatoes, the government pays to have 'em destroyed. Now, I reckon, since Centerburg doesn't need no ragweeds—well, I reckon the town ought to pay me so's they can get rid of 'em. I figger a thousand dollars and expenses, paid in cash, ought to be a fair price."

Another murmur went through the hall. The printer rose from his seat and addressed the mayor. "Mr. Mayor, a thousand dollars seems a big price for a crop of ragweed."

"These are big ragweeds, Your Honor," said Dulcy modestly.

"This sum should be paid by the national government and not by the town of Centerburg," said Lawyer Stobbs.

At this the county agent jumped to his feet and cried, "I make a motion that the town pay Dulcy. By the time that we filled out all the papers and sent them to Washington, it would be too late."

"I second that motion!" the barber spoke up.

Over the whispering of the audience the mayor called for silence and said, "A motion has been made and seconded that the town pay Dulcy Dooner one thousand dollars and expenses in cash for his ragweed plants. Because time is short and at any hour the plants may break into bloom, we will have an oral vote. All those in favor say 'aye.' "

"Aye!" said everyone.

"Anyone against?" asked the mayor. No one spoke.

114

"Majority rule," said Dulcy. "It's nice we could solve this problem so democratic like."

Then he made his way to the front of the hall and handed the mayor a paper listing his expenses:

70 bags of vitamin plant food @ $4.00 a bag	$280.00
2 assistants @ $13.00 each	26.00
Rubbing alcohol for lame back	7.13
Total expenses	$313.13

The mayor read this aloud and then said, "Added on to the thousand dollars, the total amount due to Mr. Dooner is thirteen hundred and thirteen dollars and thirteen cents."

"Homer," whispered Freddy, "there're those numbers again. That means more trouble—"

"Sh-h, Freddy," said Homer. "Look, the town treasurer and the banker are leaving to get the cash for Dulcy."

When the treasurer returned from the bank he carefully counted out thirteen hundred and thirteen dollars in bills into Dulcy's eager hand, and then just as carefully he counted out the dime and one, two, three pennies.

Dulcy stuffed the money into his pockets, and the mayor announced that after the meeting the Fire Department, and any men who might care to volunteer, would cut down the giant ragweeds and attend to the burning of the trunks and stems and blossoms.

The people applauded and cheered with relief, now that the threat had been dealt with. Life in Centerburg would not come to a sneezing halt, and business could be resumed as usual.

The mayor held up his hand for silence. "Now that we are all assembled, is there anything else that should be brought before the meeting?" he asked.

"Yes," said the town treasurer. "This business has left the town finances pretty low. We ought to discuss how to raise thirteen hundred and thirteen dollars and thirteen cents to make the budget come out right."

"We could have some new taxes!" Dulcy suggested happily. "An extra penny on ice-cream cones, a tax on movies, a penny tax here and there, and nobody'd hardly notice it."

"That's impractical," said the banker. "Think of the book-keeping trying to keep track of a penny here and there. Borrow the money from the bank and take ten years to pay it back in easy installments."

"Oh, don't do that!" Dulcy cautioned. "The town can't be payin' for *this* year's ragweed *next* year. Ya see, I got lots more seed locked up in the bank, and next year I'm countin' on a bumper crop o' giant ragweed, maybe a hundred times as much!"

"Homer," whispered Freddy, "how much is a hundred times thirteen hundred and thirteen dollars and thirteen cents?" And the whisper sounded loud over the troubled silence.

"Seems as if our troubles are never over," the mayor said sadly.

Dulcy Dooner seemed to be the only happy person in the

whole population of Centerburg. "Say!" he suggested brightly. "How about a tax on doughnuts, say, twenty-five cents a dozen?"

"No!" shouted Uncle Ulysses. "You can't get away with that, Dulcy Dooner! It's preposterous to think that the doughnut eaters of Centerburg are going to pay for your ragweed growing!"

"No need to get mad, Ulysses," said Dulcy. "Let's do this thing democratic."

Uncle Ulysses called out, "Mr. Mayor, I move that we put a tax of twenty-five cents on a dozen ragweed seed!"

"I second that motion," said the printer over Dulcy's shouts of *"No! No!"*

When the mayor called for a vote the "ayes" won, and only one person voted "no."

"Mr. Mayor," said the banker, "I move that this tax be collected immediately, in cash!"

"I second that motion," said the dentist with a chuckle.

There was plenty of chuckling and laughing throughout the hall now and everybody gleefully voted "aye."

Everybody except Dulcy Dooner. He voted "NO—O!"

"Mr. Dooner!" chuckled the mayor, "majority rule, remember? Let's be a good citizen about this!"

"You're steppin' on the minority's toes!" Dulcy shouted, but no one seemed to take notice.

The mayor appointed Uncle Ulysses Ragweed Seed Counter and made him chairman of a committee to count the seeds and collect the tax from Dulcy.

Then at last the meeting was over. The people were in a celebrating mood, the fire bell jangled merrily, and the Fire Department took over the rush job of disposing of Dulcy's plants. Groups of singing people were soon clustered about fires of burning ragweed, and it made a pretty sight, what with spotlights of the fire truck alternating red and white flashes. There was the sound of axes and saws, and then the excited cry of "Timbe-e-er!" followed by the earth trembling *crash* as a stalk of giant ragweed hit the ground.

"There goes the thirteenth ragweed plant," said Freddy with relief.

"You still worried about numbers, Freddy?" Homer asked. Then he said, "Let's go back to the bank and see how Uncle Ulysses is getting on counting ragweed seeds."

Homer and Freddy peeked through the window of the bank; it was closed up tight, and Uncle Ulysses and his committee were not inside counting seeds. Then they looked in the barbershop; the mayor, the sheriff, the barber, and Lawyer Stobbs were playing rummy, but Uncle Ulysses and his committee were not there. They finally found the seed counters in the lunchroom. Uncle Ulysses was hunched over, squinting through a magnifying glass, counting the tiny giant ragweed seeds. Every time Uncle

Ulysses counted twelve, the jeweler put down a mark, and the banker, who excelled at arithmetic, was multiplying the number of marks by twenty-five cents to find out how much the tax of twenty-five cents a dozen on ragweed seeds was mounting up to.

And Dulcy—Dulcy was there, watching like a hawk to see that nobody made mistakes in his counting or marking or multiplying. All four were so intent upon their job that they did not notice when Homer and Freddy arrived.

"Three thousand nine hundred and ninety-nine," said the jeweler.

"One, two, three, four, five, six, seven, eight, nine, ten, eleven, twelve," counted Uncle Ulysses.

"Four thousand dozen," said the jeweler.

"Four thousand dozen times twenty-five cents is one thousand dollars' tax," said the banker, "and we still have several thousand dozen seeds inside the jar to count!"

"Looks like the town is going to make money on this tax," said the jeweler.

"No, it ain't!" cried Dulcy. "Not from me it ain't!" He counted out a thousand dollars and slammed the money down on the table. "There's your durned thousand, and I'm keeping my expenses!" Then he headed for the door.

"Just a minute, Dulcy!" called Uncle Ulysses. "There are a lot more o' yer seeds to count and tax."

"My seeds, my eye!" shouted Dulcy. "You can shove 'em all in your shoe! I never want to look at another seed!" And he slammed the door of the lunchroom on his way out.

"What are you going to do with the seeds, Uncle Ulysses?" asked Homer.

"Oh, hello, boys," Uncle Ulysses said. "You're just the fellows we need here. Homer, Freddy, you finish countin' these things. It's pretty fine work and takes a young, sharp eye. We old fellows are pretty tired, and besides, we better go across to the barbershop and report to the mayor."

Homer and Freddy started counting and the committee went off to make its report.

"Gosh, Homer," Freddy complained, "there's still thousands of seeds here to count and it will take all night! I don't see why they have to be counted anyway. Dulcy isn't going to pay any more tax on them."

"It's important to count them, though," said Homer. "You know something, Freddy, counting and keeping track of every single one of these seeds is just about the most important job in Centerburg."

"More important than being mayor?" asked Freddy.

"Sure," said Homer, "because if one single seed got lost, it might grow into a giant-size ragweed."

"Just one giant-size ragweed might not make everybody sneeze so bad, Homer," said Freddy.

"Yes, it would too," Homer said. "If the pollen from one giant ragweed mixed itself with all the common wild ragweed hereabouts, then the next year there would be hybrid ragweed every place."

"Gosh, Homer, just like hybrid corn. The hybrid ragweeds would be bigger than ever!" said Freddy.

Homer nodded his head gravely. "Just supposing somebody subversive, like an enemy, was to capture these seeds, Freddy, and plant them some night right next to the White House and the Capitol!"

"And the President and the senators and representatives all started sneezing with hay fever!" Freddy said.

"Yup," said Homer. "The President couldn't hold press conferences and the senators couldn't make speeches, and I just

123

guess the government would come to a stop. Everything would get tangled up and disrupt the country. You see, counting these seeds is super important!" And he picked up the magnifying glass and started to count giant ragweed seeds.

Over across the town square in the barbershop, Uncle Ulysses and the committee had joined the game of rummy, after they had reported to the mayor.

"It's your turn to draw a card, Ulysses," said the sheriff.

"Queen of seeds," said Uncle Ulysses, turning over a card. "Zeus!" he said. "I keep seein' those things in front o' my eyes. Reminds me, I better call up the lunchroom and see how Homer and Freddy are gettin' along." He picked up the phone and gave the number. "Hello, Homer? How're you makin' out? Still have a lot to count, eh?" Uncle Ulysses listened for a minute and then he said, "We thought we'd just lock 'em up in the bank again. Nobody would ever think of plantin' a crop of ragweeds—except Dulcy, that is. If they knew what they was plantin', they wouldn't." Uncle Ulysses listened again and stopped smiling; then he looked worried. "Homer," he said, trying to control his voice, "you just keep right on countin' and be extra careful not to lose a single seed. Don't you worry, son, we'll talk it over and think of a way to get rid of 'em somehow." Uncle Ulysses hung up the receiver and went back to the rummy game with terror in his eyes and fear in his heart.

"Men," said Uncle Ulysses gravely, "we've got to think hard or this country will be one big sneeze clear from the Atlantic to the Pacific coast! Why, one single enemy plane could sow those seeds from New York to San Francisco in a couple of hours!"

"What are you raving about, Ulysses?" asked the barber.

"It's the strain of counting all those little seeds that's got him upset, I guess," said the banker.

"I'm not ravin'!" said Uncle Ulysses, glaring wildly at the rummy players. "You men put down your cards and listen to me. We have to think and think fast of a way to get rid of those seeds. If the wrong kind of people were to get hold of 'em, it would mean the ruin of this country!"

"Shucks, Ulysses, we're going to lock 'em up again in the safe deposit vault, so stop worrying and let's get on with the game!" said the printer.

"Stop being so—so—so complacent," Uncle Ulysses sputtered. "Banks get robbed almost every day and you know it." Then he looked over his shoulder and leaned way over close and whispered hoarsely, "And the kind of people I mean wouldn't stop at nothing!"

"I'll lock them ragweed seeds in the jail," said the sheriff triumphantly. "That'll stop 'em!"

"Rubbish," said Uncle Ulysses. "As many as twenty people have broken out of your jail, Sheriff, and it's a durned sight easier to break in. Besides, the jail has got mice. Suppose some mouse was to take some of those seeds home to a hole in the ground to feed his family? Then where'd we be? Right back where we were with Dulcy, only this time we might not act in

125

time." Uncle Ulysses was excited now and he shouted, "Bees and bugs! We'll have to get rid of 'em so they won't find 'em! I tell ya, men, if the pollen from just one of these giant ragweeds gets loose and mixes with our wild ragweeds, we'll have hybrid ragweeds bigger even than the giant ragweeds."

All the men finally realized the seriousness of the situation, and they sat glancing uneasily at one another. The mayor was the first to move; he dashed over to the window and looked across the deserted square at the lunchroom.

"There's no use worrying those two boys about this," he said. "But we had better post a guard outside while they finish their counting. Sheriff," he ordered, "you take your gun and cover the front entrance. And Biggs," he said, handing the barber his keys, "you'll find a revolver in the upper right-hand drawer of my desk. You guard the back entrance. The rest of us will stay here and try to dope out a solution to this problem. In case of trouble, fire a shot into the air and we'll be right over to help out."

The sheriff and the barber went out the door, and the rest of the men drew their chairs up close together for a conference.

"Now then," said the mayor, "let's decide what to do."

Nobody said anything for some minutes. They all sat thinking. Then Uncle Ulysses said, "Well, let's decide."

"I've heard tell that birds sometimes plant seeds in out-of-the-way places," said the banker.

"Yeh, birds and mice and bugs. We have to dispose of them some way so they won't get at them," said Uncle Ulysses.

"The most important thing is to keep these ragweed seeds from falling into the hands of enemy agents," said Lawyer Stobbs. "Sneezing could seriously impair the functioning of the executive and the judicial as well as the legislative branches of our federal government."

"What can we do with them? Where can we put them? How can we get rid of them so not one seed can fall into the hands of some enemy agent? Or mouse? Or bird? Or bug?" asked Uncle Ulysses, pacing up and down.

"The bank wouldn't be safe," said the banker.

"It wouldn't be safe to bury the seeds," said the printer.

"If we hid them inside a mattress, the mice would find them," said the mayor.

"I was thinking, if we were to hide them up at the very top of the courthouse tower it might be a good place, but the—"

"Pigeons!" everybody said at once.

"Of course," said Uncle Ulysses, "if we had the time, we could have a special burglar-bug-bird-and-mouse-proof container made to order, something like the Time Capsule that they buried at the World's Fair. That would take months, and it would be a tremendous responsibility to guard those seeds day and night until then."

"I'm for calling in the FBI right now," said the banker. "There isn't a single place under the earth, on the earth, or a steeple over the earth that's a safe place to hide those seeds."

"The ocean!" shouted Uncle Ulysses. "The Atlantic Ocean!

The sheriff could take the seeds to Atlantic City and hire a boat to take him to a nice deep spot. Then he could toss the ragweed seeds overboard, and that would be that."

"That's it, Ulysses," said the mayor. "There's a train for the East that goes through here at twelve-forty tonight. We'll send the sheriff to Atlantic City to sink those seeds!"

"I've got a metal cashbox with a lock and a nice handle," said the banker. "The sheriff could carry the seeds in that and handcuff it to his wrist, so nobody could steal it on the train."

"And I've got some heavy lead type to put in the box just to make sure it'll sink," said the printer.

"Fine," said the mayor. "You two fellows get the box and weight it with type, and Lawyer Stobbs, you relieve the sheriff at the front of the lunchroom, so he can go home and pack. Ulysses and myself will call the station and make reservations for the sheriff on the twelve-forty."

In shortly less than half an hour the box was ready and back at the barbershop; and five minutes later the sheriff came in carrying his bag, all packed and ready to go. He pulled out a pair of handcuffs, and one side he fastened to his wrist and the other he snapped through the handle of the box.

"You mustn't forget to unfasten yourself before you toss the box, Sheriff," said the printer with a smile.

"This is no time for joking," said the mayor severely. "Now, Sheriff, you realize how much depends on you. Don't speak to strangers on the train," he cautioned, "and as soon as you get to Atlantic City, hire a boat and go out and sink the seeds."

"You can depend on me, Mayor!" promised the sheriff.

"All right," said the mayor, "let's go over to the lunchroom and pick up the seeds."

The mayor led the way across the town square, followed by Uncle Ulysses, the sheriff, the banker, and the printer. Lawyer Stobbs, gun in hand, met them at the door of the lunchroom.

"Everything all right inside?" Uncle Ulysses asked in a whisper.

"Yes," whispered the lawyer, "I think they're all finished with counting. Sh-h! What's that!" he said, pointing his gun out into the shadows of the square.

After a tense moment of waiting, the postmaster's dog came up wagging his tail. Everybody relaxed and Uncle Ulysses chuckled, "That dog can smell doughnuts cookin' a mile away! Come on. Let's go inside and pack up the seeds and get something to eat. I'm hungry." He opened the door and went in, followed by all the men and the postmaster's dog.

"Hello, boys. All through counting, I see," said the mayor.

"Ah-h!" exclaimed Uncle Ulysses. "Very thoughtful of you, Homer, to make some doughnuts. The sheriff can take some with him for a snack on the train, and we're all pretty hungry right this minute." He paused to admire his automatic doughnut machine make doughnuts. And as he watched, the machine stopped.

Uncle Ulysses, who had started passing out the hot doughnuts, said, "You didn't mix up enough batter. You should have made more."

"But, Uncle Ulysses, we only meant to make a dozen," said Homer.

"Yeah," said Freddy, who had been counting the doughnuts as they came out of the machine. "We only meant to make a dozen." Then he added miserably, "But it turned out to be thirteen!"

"Well, there's enough to go around, so help yourselves, everybody," Uncle Ulysses offered.

"But Uncle Ulysses—" said Homer.

"Freddy, you go to the back door and call the barber," Uncle Ulysses said, suddenly remembering that the barber was still guarding the rear.

"Uncle Ulysses—" Homer started to say.

"Let's get the seeds in the box and locked up," said the mayor, taking a bite of doughnut, "and then I'd like a cup of coffee."

Freddy came back with the barber, and Uncle Ulysses handed him a doughnut. Then he turned to Homer. "Get the ragweed seeds, son, and put them in that box the sheriff's got danglin' from his wrist."

"But, Uncle Ulysses," said Homer, "that's what I've been trying to tell you!" Then he asked, "Have you ever heard of a berry growing into a berry bush after it had once been cooked into a pie?"

Uncle Ulysses had his mouth full of doughnut and so did all the other men, so they all shook their heads "no."

"Have you ever heard of a nut growing into a nut tree after being baked into a cookie?" Homer asked.

And again all the men nodded their heads, because they were chewing doughnut and trying to swallow.

"Popcorn won't grow after it's been popped either," said Freddy, "because I tried it once."

Uncle Ulysses gulped and said, "Homer, you're a good boy, it's gettin' late, and you and Freddy run along home now."

After Homer and Freddy had gone the mayor fed the rest of his doughnut to the postmaster's dog. So did Uncle Ulysses and the barber and the jeweler, the printer, the banker, the sheriff, and Lawyer Stobbs. Then they fed him the rest of the doughnuts and watched silently while he ate up every last crumb. As the last crumb disappeared the sheriff said, "There goes my trip to Atlantic City."

And the barber said, "From now on, every time I look at that dog or even mail a letter, I'll probably have to sn-sn-s-s-ss*harah-choowh!*"

EVER SO MUCH MORE SO

EVER SO MUCH MORE SO

THE EARLY afternoon spring sunshine came peeping into the lunchroom and reflected off the stainless steel trim of Uncle Ulysses' unpredictable automatic doughnut machine.

The sun reflected off the shiny metal and right into the eyes of Uncle Ulysses, who was settled comfortably at the counter, having an after-lunch chat with the sheriff and the judge.

Uncle Ulysses blinked his eyes and thought, "I'll have to get up and go all the way outside to wind that awning down. Ought to put a motor on it," he thought, "with a button under the counter, to save all those steps and all the winding." Then he yawned out loud and shifted his position just enough to allow the reflection to go over his shoulder.

"Put a button on it," he said, thinking out loud, much to the confusion of the judge and the sheriff.

"Put what?" asked Homer, who was wiping crumbs off the counter.

"Oh, yes, Homer," said Uncle Ulysses with a start. "Put the awning down, like a good fellow, would you please?"

"Okay, Uncle Ulysses," said Homer and, after wiping a pile of crumbs off the counter into his apron, he hustled outside and shook them onto the curb. He watched while the Centerburg town-hall pigeons started arriving to eat crumbs, then hustled back across the walk and wound down the awning.

"Thank you, Homer," said Uncle Ulysses as Homer came back into the lunchroom.

"Everything look feacepul—I mean peaceful—and law abidin' out on the square?" the sheriff demanded of Homer.

"Dulcy Dooner is headed in this direction," Homer said.

"Ah-h!" said the judge. *"That* exceedingly uncooperative citizen of our community!"

They all turned and watched through the window of the lunchroom while Dulcy paused next to the monument. The sheriff bristled when Dulcy struck a match on the bronze tablet, casually lit his pipe, and flipped the burned match in the general direction of the statue of "Peace." Then he came on toward the lunchroom, detouring slightly in order to scuffle through the crumbs and frighten a few pigeons.

Slam! went the door of the lunchroom as Dulcy came in. But the sheriff, the judge, Uncle Ulysses, and Homer hardly jumped. They all knew how Dulcy closed doors.

"What are you up to these days, Dulcy?" asked the sheriff, eying Dulcy carefully as though expecting to find something like packages of strange seeds or bottles of elixir sticking out of his pockets.

"Always suspectin' me!" complained Dulcy. "Sheriff, you're the most suspicious guy in the state of Ohio!"

"In view of several unfortunate occurrences attributable

135

directly to certain actions of one Dulcy Dooner, I am of the opinion," the judge proclaimed in his usual pompous way, "that the suspicions of our sheriff are entirely justified."

"Good afternoon, my friends!" said a strange voice, and the judge, the sheriff, Uncle Ulysses, Dulcy Dooner, and Homer turned to see a stranger walk in the door. He had a case under one arm and a folding stand under the other.

"Good afternoon, my friends," he repeated. "You are without doubt the most fortunate people in the world—and in just one minute, yes, one short sixty seconds of your valuable time, I am going to make you even more fortunate . . . thankful that I have come to you with this sensational introductory offer!"

The stranger, after introducing himself as Professor Ear, "Professor Atmos *P. H.* Ear," talked on and on, scarcely stopping to take a breath, and at the same time managed to shut the door, tip his hat, unfold his stand, set up his case carefully, and take off his gloves, smiling sweetly all the while.

"I have in here," he continued, tapping the lid of his case, "one of the wonders of the world! Yes, my friends, and you *are* my very good friends, in just one minute I am going to reveal to you a product and make you an offer that will change your life, *if* you are the kind of people that get a *bang* out of life," he exclaimed, emphasizing the *bang* with a flourish and swat of his gloves on top of his case. "You are the ones, yes, the very people, that will have the good sense, the intelligence, imagination, ability, good judgment, and love of the finer things in life to apply this amazing product to obtain the beneficial blessings, the sense of well being, and complete, yes, complete, satisfaction that this remarkable product has the ability to impart to each and every one."

"We don't want any o'—" Dulcy started to interrupt.

"It is my honor," continued the professor, loud enough to be heard above Dulcy's interruption, "to bring to you this fabulously amazing and most phenomenal product, and its name is"—he paused dramatically, snapping free the fastenings of the case and throwing up the cover—"its name is EVERSOMUCH MORE-SO!"

The judge, the sheriff, Uncle Ulysses, Dulcy, and Homer all stared at the cans displayed so suddenly before their eyes.

"What—?" Uncle Ulysses started to ask.

"Ah-h, *what?"* echoed the stranger. "Ah-h, yes, my good friends, I can see the question in your friendly faces. *What* is this remarkable EVERSOMUCH MORE-SO, and *what* can this phenomenal EVERSOMUCH MORE-SO do for *me?* In just one minute, just thirty short seconds, I am going to demonstrate to you and to prove to you without the shadow of a doubt that this product can accomplish wondrous things.

"Each and every can," said the professor, picking up a can and continuing without a pause, "yes, *each* and *every* can comes complete with a handy adjustable top. A slight twist to either left or right opens the tiny holes in the cap, making EVERSOMUCH MORE-SO readily accessible for instantaneous application.

"Now for the purposes of our demonstration," the professor continued quickly, "we shall use these delicious-looking doughnuts. Young man," he said to Homer, "if you will be so kind as to pass the tray, and if you gentlemen," he requested, bowing low, "would be so kind as to take two doughnuts . . ."

While Homer passed the tray and everyone took two doughnuts, one in each hand, the professor said, "Now, my friends, we are ready to—uht, uht, sonny, don't forget me!" And before Homer could pass the tray the professor speared two doughnuts on the end of his cane.

The judge and Uncle Ulysses exchanged looks, and the sheriff was about to ask, "When—?"

"Now," said the professor loudly, banging on his case for undivided attention, "now we are ready to proceed with our demonstration. Yes, in just one minute, only sixty seconds—but first," said the professor, picking up a can of EVERSOMUCH MORE-SO, "I shall acquaint you with this wondrous product."

The judge, the sheriff, Uncle Ulysses, Homer, and Dulcy all leaned closer, each with both eyes watching the professor twist the adjustable can top, and each with doughnuts in both hands.

"As I proceed, young man," the professor said to Homer, "please pour cups of your delicious coffee for everyone here."

"Ahuumph!" the judge cleared his throat restlessly.

"A cup of coffee costs—". Uncle Ulysses began.

"Everybody eat the doughnut in his right hand!" the professor commanded loudly. "Delicious—uhm-m? Simply delicious," he declared, taking a dainty bite from the one on the tip of his cane. Having safely stopped all interruptions with large bites of doughnut, the professor continued in a low, confiding voice, "EVERSOMUCH MORE-SO is a truly remarkable product."

He shook some on his doughnut and swung it in front of the noses of his audience, on the tip of his cane, for all to see. "Remarkable, you say!" interpreted the professor, loudly enough to be heard over sounds coming from behind mouthfuls of doughnut. "Yes, my friends, EVERSOMUCH MORE-SO is *invisible!* And what's more, EVERSOMUCH MORE-SO cannot be smelled," he said, passing the can quickly beneath every nose. "You cannot feel it, and you cannot see it," he added, rubbing his fingertips and then wiggling the can close to his ear.

"Pass the coffee, young man!" he commanded Homer and quickly continued his speech. "EVERSOMUCH MORE-SO is *absolutely invisible* to the naked eye, odorless to the human nose, soundless to the—young man, don't forget the cream and sugar —as I was saying, soundless to the unassisted perceptibilities of the human ear, undetected, by itself, by the sensitive human nerves of touch, and what is more, EVERSOMUCH MORE-SO, taken from the can in its natural unadulterated state, is completely tasteless to the sensitive taste buds of the human tongue.

"Now you are about to ask," the professor said, "why should we be interested in this product we cannot see, smell, taste, hear, or feel? But *watch closely!* Sprinkle a small amount of EVERSOMUCH MORE-SO in your good aromatic cup of coffee—so!

Immediately, yes, my friends, *im-me-e-ediately,* that good aromatic cup of coffee becomes *ever so much more so!* Yes, indeed, and after sprinkling a few drops of this remarkable, invisible, tasteless, odorless, textureless, absolutely soundless product on the delicious doughnut you hold in your hand, that delicious doughnut becomes immediately *ever so much more so* delicious!"

The can was passed to Dulcy and on to the judge, from the judge to the sheriff, on to Uncle Ulysses, and last of all to Homer. Everyone shook out a small amount of EVERSOMUCH MORE-SO into his cup of coffee and onto his second doughnut.

Everybody began tasting carefully, exchanging glances, tasting once more, and nodding solemnly, while the professor talked on and on.

"Yes, my friends, that is indeed the most *ever so much more so* delicious doughnut and the best, yes, without doubt, the most *ever so much more so* aromatic cup of coffee you have ever tasted."

Everyone was nodding in agreement and enjoying his doughnut and coffee—everybody but Homer, who was tasting his coffee and making miserable faces. Finally he asked, "What if you don't like coffee? Does—?"

"DOES EVERSOMUCH MORE-SO work on *everything,* this young man wants to know?" the professor said quickly. "Ah, but yes!" he shouted. "*Everything.* It will make a rose smell ever so much more lovely, curly hair ever so much more curly, beautiful music ever so much more beautiful. Yes, my friends, surely you are all

142

intelligent enough to realize the far-reaching possibilities of EVERSOMUCH MORE-SO! It comes to you in this convenient can, put up under the most sanitary conditions by the famous Doctor Forscyth Eversomuch in his great open-air laboratory. One can, yes, one single can, lasts a lifetime. After purchasing one can of EVERSOMUCH MORE-SO, a man can rest assured that he will never again want for another can of EVERSOMUCH MORE-SO. It will keep just as fresh, just as free from impurities, just as potent inside the can as the day it was packed. And now for the amazing price of fifty cents, only four bits, one-half of one dollar, a lifetime can of EVERSOMUCH MORE-SO is yours. This is one of the good things of the earth, men. Now don't miss this golden opportunity to own a convenient can of it for this amazing price of fifty cents."

The sheriff counted out fifty cents, the judge bought a can, so did Uncle Ulysses. Even Dulcy borrowed half a dollar from the judge and bought a can.

As the professor prepared to snap shut his case Homer asked, "If you don't like coffee and you put EVERSOMUCH MORE-SO in it, then will you not like coffee *ever so much more so?*"

"How would you like," the professor asked, "a nice fast kick— eherump—would you like a nice free can of EVERSOMUCH MORE-SO?" And he quickly tossed a can to Homer, snapped up his case, hooked his cane over his arm, pulled on his gloves, tipped his hat, and was out of the door and away in an instant.

"G'by," said Dulcy abruptly. "I'm gonna try this stuff on something."

"Me too," said the sheriff.

"Good day, Ulysses," said the judge, remembering to be polite.

"Um-m," answered Uncle Ulysses absent-mindedly, for he was carefully selecting two doughnuts.

When he and Homer were alone Uncle Ulysses put the two doughnuts on two plates. One he left plain and the other he sprinkled liberally with EVERSOMUCH MORE-SO. Then he tasted, first one, then the other, the one with, the other without. He stroked his chin, then called Homer, and they both tasted.

"I'll be durned," said Uncle Ulysses finally.

"You know, Uncle Ulysses," Homer said, "nobody paid for coffee and doughnuts this afternoon."

"I'll be durned," Uncle Ulysses repeated. *"Ever so much more so!"*

The following Thursday Uncle Ulysses sat slumped on his stool behind the counter when the judge walked in.

"Judge," Uncle Ulysses asked sleepily, "do you notice anything different about me?"

The judge looked Uncle Ulysses over carefully and said, "I notice a marked tendency toward sleepiness."

"Uh-uh-uh," nodded Uncle Ulysses with a yawn, "that's what Aggie says. Says I'm lazier than ever—*ever so much more so,* she says. That's not so, Judge. But I just can't seem to sleep at night any more. I put some EVERSOMUCH MORE-SO on my inner-spring mattress to make it softer."

"And did it?" asked the judge.

"Yes," nodded Uncle Ulysses, "but I spilled some of the stuff on one of the springs that had a slight squeak and it seemed to start squeaking *ever so much more so*. Can't sleep a wink in that bed. Hello, Sheriff," he added as the sheriff came in, looking flustered and red in the face.

"Gentlemen," the judge said solemnly, "I fear that some grave metamorphosis of cerebral or of physical characteristics has erupted within my innermost self. In fact," he said pompously, "I am just exactly like myself, only *ever so much more so*."

"Tomesimes," said the sheriff sadly, "I wix my mords all up, but sis thuff ixxes 'em mup so I don't even snow what I'm krying to snay!"

"I think," said Uncle Ulysses gravely, "that we are imaginin' the whole thing. A man just *can't* be more like himself than he is already. Let's ask Dulcy," suggested Uncle Ulysses.

And indeed there was Dulcy, stamping across the grass in the square. He stumbled over a "Keep Off the Grass" sign, let out a loud bellow, picked up the sign and threw it in the general direction of "Peace." "Peace" went kabonk! as the sign smacked into her. After knocking over a trash can, Dulcy came on toward the lunchroom.

"He's *ever so much more so,* all right. Been eatin' it every day, I bet," said Uncle Ulysses while the sheriff and judge nodded.

Slam! went the door as Dulcy came in. Homer and Freddy

came in soon after and looked concernedly at ever so drowsy Uncle Ulysses, at the ever so pompous judge, the ever so flustered and suspicious sheriff, and the *ever so much more so* uncooperative citizen named Dulcy Dooner.

"How *you* feelin', Homer?" Uncle Ulysses asked.

"Just fine, Uncle Ulysses," Homer answered. "You look sleepy, Uncle Ulysses. Got spring fever?"

"What did you do with your can of EVERSOMUCH MORE-SO, Homer?" asked Uncle Ulysses, trying to keep awake and unconcerned.

"Oh, *that* stuff," said Homer. "Freddy and I put a lot of it on my radio to improve the reception. It seemed a little better but it seemed to make ever so much more static and interference too. So we took a screw driver and pried the top off the EVERSOMUCH MORE-SO can, just to see what was inside."

"Yes?" everybody asked.

"Yes," said Homer.

"It was empty," Freddy said with a shrug.

"That stuff is invisible," Dulcy reminded.

"Well, it was an empty can!" said Freddy defiantly.

"And what could be more empty than an EVERSOMUCH MORE-SO empty can?" asked Homer.

"We've been dindled, doggonit—I mean swindled," howled the sheriff.

"Our fertile imaginations have led us astray," pronounced the judge.

"The professor took us, all right," chuckled Uncle Ulysses, seeming to come more awake of a sudden.

"Here, Judge," said Dulcy, handing over his can of EVERSO-MUCH MORE-SO. "Now we're even and I don't owe you fifty cents."

"Help yourselves to doughnuts, boys," Uncle Ulysses said solicitously, the way he always did before asking a favor.

"Boys," he said, "we can't let this affair come to the attention of Grampa Hercules or we'll never hear the end of it."

Homer hesitated until both he and Freddy had helped themselves to doughnuts and then said, "He already knows."

"What?" cried the sheriff and Uncle Ulysses.

"Yep. I put the top back on the can and decided to give it to Grampa Herc. It's the sort of thing he would appreciate ever so much, you know," Homer said.

"And what did the gold oat—I mean, what did the *old goat* say?" demanded the sheriff, clearly expecting the worst.

"He said it beat all what the world was coming to, didn't he, Freddy? And he said," Homer continued, "that it used to come in bulk when he was young, and lots cheaper too. Nobody bothered to give it a fancy name or put it in a package with an adjustable top."

"Continue, young man," the judge suggested.

"Well," Homer said, "he allowed as how he'd never tried this *packaged* kind of EVERSOMUCH MORE-SO and he had a feeling he'd like to see if it was just as strong as the old-fashioned kind. So I sold him *my* can for a dollar."

"That's my nephew, and more so," said Uncle Ulysses.

"We been swindled!" repeated the sheriff. "I shoulda locked that fella up!"

"*Entirely* outside the law!" the judge proclaimed.

"Helloooo, everybody!" said Grampa Hercules, letting himself in the door.

Uncle Ulysses sighed and wondered to himself how more so Grampa Herc could possibly get.

"How do you feel, Hercules?" the judge inquired.

"Never felt so good in my whole life!" answered Grampa Herc.

"Okay, what did you do with it?" demanded Dulcy.

Grampa Herc looked puzzled; then he said, "Oh, you mean the stuff in the can, the EVERSOMUCH MORE-SO. Wu-a-ll, you know, I got to thinkin'. An old fella like me ain't got long to spend in these parts. I can use up a lot o' time sprinklin' a bit on this and that, here and there. I thought to myself, what's one big, all-fired-honest-to-crawfish, powerful, important way to use up a lifetime supply of EVERSOMUCH MORE-SO? I thought and I thought, and finally it come to me. I went out in my backyard and hunted up a nice soft spot of black earth. Then I started to shake that stuff on that wonderful earth as hard as my arm could shake. I shook until my arm got tired, and I reckon the can was just about empty. Then I took a screw driver and pried off the lid and poured the EVERSOMUCH MORE-SO can full of water, and *do you know,* that was the *dampest,* the *soakenest,* wringin' wettest sloppin'-to-goodness can of water I ever laid eyes on!"

"Yes?" said Uncle Ulysses.

"Yep!" said Grampa Herc. "And then I dumped that EVER-SOMUCH MORE-SO soakingest water onto that good old earth and watched it soak in, right down to the core—somewhere halfway between here and China. Then I looked around me and noticed how green the grass looked—trees budding, birds singing, and I felt good all over! See, look out there in the square—just like I'm tellin' you. It's a great old world!" shouted Grampa Herc, leaping up and clicking his heels, "and what's more, it's getting better all the time! So long, everybody!"

Uncle Ulysses, the sheriff, the judge, Dulcy, Homer, and Freddy all walked out into the square in the nice warm spring sunshine.

"Do you think I ought to give this fifty cents back to Grampa Herc?" asked Homer, holding out half a dollar.

"You just loan that to me, Homer," said Dulcy, making a grab, "and I'll buy my can back from the judge. You can owe Grampa Hercules the *other* fifty cents."

"Homer," said Uncle Ulysses, "run back to the lunchroom and bring a screw driver from the tool box. Freddy, you go along and bring a pitcher of water."

Uncle Ulysses was scraping up a nice soft absorbent spot under an old maple right near the statue of "Peace."

"You know," he said, "it's really a waste of time to shake it on. We'll just fill it right up to the top and let it keep a-runnin' over and soakin' in!"

PIE AND PUNCH AND
YOU-KNOW-WHATS

PIE AND PUNCH AND YOU-KNOW-WHATS

UNCLE ULYSSES stood near the door of his lunchroom, leaning on his new automatic jukebox. While he peered out across the square toward the lighted windows of the Centerburg Public Library, his face gradually changed from pink to a deep beet-red. It turned lavender for a fleeting moment, then faded off into a flickering grassy green color. Uncle Ulysses was not feeling sick, but he'd been changing colors like this for several days now—ever since he'd acquired his beautiful new automatic jukebox. The new jukebox had brilliant lights inside that automatically changed color every few seconds, and anybody or anything that came within ten feet of the jukebox automatically changed color too.

No, Uncle Ulysses was not feeling sick, but he was feeling impatient, and just as he—and the jukebox—automatically turned lavender for the seventeenth time, the door opened, and in walked Homer and Freddy.

"Hi, Uncle Ulysses!" Homer greeted. "Sorry we're late. We picked out a lot of books this evening, because the library's going to be closed for two weeks."

"The librarian is going away on a vacation," Freddy explained, "so we picked out enough books to last until she comes back."

"I heard that she was going to Yellowstone Park with the sixth-grade teacher," said Uncle Ulysses, who kept pretty close track of things like that.

"Yep," said Homer, "and she promised to send us a postcard with a picture of Old Faithful on it."

"That'll be nice," said Uncle Ulysses, listening politely. Then he said, "Boys, I'm goin' over to the barbershop for a spell, so you two fellows help yourself to doughnuts and look after things while I'm gone."

"Okay, Uncle Ulysses," Homer said, and then he watched patiently while Uncle Ulysses went from one of his automatic gadgets to the next—first turning them on and then turning them off, just to make sure they would stop. It was a slight nervous habit that Uncle Ulysses had developed of late, and it seemed to be more noticeable right before he planned to leave Homer in charge of the lunchroom. He checked them off one by one—waffle irons, toaster, doughnut machine, dishwasher. Last of all, he walked over to check his new automatic jukebox. He gave it an affectionate pat (it was a pink pat, because the automatic lights happened to be pink at the moment). He punched a button to select a number called "Boogie Woogie Symphony," and dropped a nickel (a green one) into the green slot of the jukebox. There was a *cl-l-lick!* and mysteriously and silently the record that Uncle Ulysses had selected slid out of a large stack and began to spin.

"Golly," said Freddy, "it seems almost like magic!"

Uncle Ulysses smiled orangely, and they all three stood entranced, listening to the beautiful full-bodied tones of a boogie-woogie symphony orchestra.

"It almost seems to hypmatize you!" Homer exclaimed as he listened to the music and watched the record spin and the lights shift slowly from one color to another.

Uncle Ulysses nodded proudly, and as the music ended on an odd minor boogie-woogie note, he watched tensely while some mysterious automatic fingers inside the jukebox silently slipped the record back into the stack.

"There," he said, visibly relieved, "that *works* perfectly, and it *stops* perfectly! Here are a couple of nickels, boys, you can have some music while I'm gone."

Homer and Freddy thanked Uncle Ulysses, and after he had gone off to the barbershop they sat silently for some moments, watching the colored lights inside the jukebox slowly change from one color to another.

"Hawh!" Freddy looked at Homer and smiled weakly. "You sure look funny, sitting over there in that green light!"

"Hawh yourself," Homer answered. "You don't look so hot either, specially when you're turning blue all over! C'mon Freddy, have a doughnut, and let's look at our library books."

Homer and Freddy had finished their doughnuts and were trying to decide which books to read first and which to save until last when a stranger opened the door and stalked into the lunchroom.

"Good evening," he said softly, brandishing a flat parcel and turning slowly from rosy pink to deep purple, along with the parcel and the lights in the jukebox.

"I have brought a recording to put in your jukebox," he said, furiously fumbling with the strings and paper of his parcel. "It will be number one on the *bit*—" The stranger broke off suddenly and stood quietly in order to change colors and to compose himself.

Homer and Freddy changed colors, too, while they watched and waited silently.

Then the stranger, having calmed down to some extent, repeated, "It will be number one on the *Hit Parade!*" He finished undoing his package and produced a recording, which he carelessly tossed almost to the ceiling. Then he stood motionless, his arms dangling limp at his sides, watching it drop. The record landed with a *crash!* on the lunchroom floor. Homer and Freddy gasped, and the stranger laughed.

"Unbreakable!" he said, chuckling. He picked up the record and bent it almost double. "Absolutely, disgustingly unbreakable! I've *tried* to break it—goodness knows I've *tried*," he said as though he were apologizing to Homer and Freddy. He then turned purposefully and unlocked the glass front of the jukebox. "I'll put it right here between 'Boogie Woogie Symphony' and 'Boogie Woogie Polka,' " he said, sliding the record into the stack. Then he quickly snapped the glass case shut and locked it with a flourish.

"There!" he said with great relief and a slight change of hue, "that's that!"

The two boys felt relieved too. They had gotten over being startled by the sudden appearance of this odd stranger. Homer, remembering his job, put down the book he had been holding and went behind the counter.

"Would you care for a snack to eat, sir? A sandwich and a cup of coffee?" he asked. "Some nice fresh doughn—"

"Uht! Uht! Uht! Uht!" the stranger interrupted, wagging his finger violently, before Homer could finish saying "doughnuts."

"I *never, never* eat them," he confided. Then, leaning way over, he whispered, "They're positively full of *holes,* you know! They're simply full of *whole holes!*"

Homer thought about that for a moment and then shrugged his shoulders. "How about a piece of pie, sir?" he asked pleasantly.

"Oh, me, oh, my!" the stranger gasped. "I *never, never* eat *hip!*" He hiccupped. "I never eat *hip* pie, because the very thought of *hip* pie makes me *hip* hiccup!"

Homer quickly filled a glass with water and handed it to the stranger. "Hold your breath and count to ten while you drink this!" he commanded. And the stranger meekly did as he was told. "That always cures my hiccups," Homer explained.

"It cures my hiccups too," said Freddy, "but I don't get 'em from thinking about p—"

"Uht! Uht! Uht!" sputtered the stranger, waving an arm wildly

and almost dropping the glass. He looked reproachfully at
Freddy and then turned to Homer. "Thank you, young man, for
curing my hiccups. I must go now, I really must be going," he
said, turning toward the door. He appeared anxious to be gone
before something dreadful could happen.

"Hey, mister," Freddy called, "you forgot to put a name for
the new record here next to the selector buttons!"

"Oh," said the stranger, pausing with his hand on the door,
"it hasn't any name. It's—ah—just one of those things. And by

160

the way," he added, *"don't play it!* I beg of you to never set needle to its black unbreakable surface, and *never* let its sounds escape from this beautiful, gaudy jukebox." The stranger paused while Homer and Freddy nodded and gulped.

Suddenly, without the least trace of humor, the stranger laughed, "Hah, hah, hah!" and changed to a lovely shade of blue-green. *"But you will,"* he whispered, taking on an amethyst tinge. "Now, good night, my proud, parturient pair of panted Pandoras!"

Then the door closed ever so grass-green and softly.

"That character," said Freddy after a long silence, "could make some little squirrel very happy. What did he mean, Homer, when he called us a 'proud, parturient pair of panted Pandoras'? A Pandora is an animal, isn't it? Why did that screwball call us a couple of proud animals with pants on?"

"You're thinking of panda, Freddy," said Homer. "But *Pandora* is a girl's name."

"He called us *girls!*" cried Freddy, doubling his fists in frustration. "Now, how's that for a character! He calls you a girl with words over your word level!"

"He didn't exactly call us girls, Freddy," Homer said thoughtfully. "At least not just *any* old kind of girl. Pandora was somebody famous—like Pocahontas or Molly Pitcher. Seems as though I've read something about her doing something very special, but I can't remember what. We have to find out exactly what this dame Pandora did before we'll know exactly what he meant. It might be a sort of a clue, Freddy, and that word 'parturient,' mebbe we ought to find out what *that* means. I'll match you, Freddy, to see who runs over to the library to look 'em up," Homer suggested, producing a nickel from a pocket of his blue jeans and giving it an expert flip.

"Okay," Freddy agreed, producing his nickel and flipping too.

"They're both heads," said Homer when they had uncovered their coins, "so you have to look 'em up, Freddy."

"Well, all right, if you think it's absolutely necessary, Homer, but I still think the guy was nuts. I'll look up 'parturient' in the dictionary, but where will I look to find out about that Pandora dame?"

"She might be in the dictionary too," Homer said, "but if she isn't there, you'll have to ask the librarian where to find her."

"All that trouble to find out about some silly dame!" said Freddy disgustedly. Then he grumbled something about screwballs in general and went scuffling out of the door, muttering, " 'Proud, parturient pair of panted Pandoras!' Cripes! The guy musta had 'Ps' for supper!"

"Did you get the dope, Freddy?" Homer asked expectantly when Freddy came scuffling back into the lunchroom.

"Yeah," said Freddy, assuming the look of a martyr because of all the mental effort he had just put forth. "She was a dame, and she had a box that she wasn't supposed to open the lid of, or let anything out of. And she did. And what came out was a lot of some kind of trouble things that must be extinct by now, because the whole thing happened such a long time ago. And 'parturient,' " Freddy continued, "means 'just about to let something out.' So you see, Homer, first he tells us not to, then he tells us we will, then he tells us we shouldn't, and then the screwball says we're 'parturient,' and just about to! The guy was nuts, Homer. I'll flip you to see who plays the record first."

"Well," said Homer doubtfully, "mebbe we better not—not until Uncle Ulysses comes back, anyway."

"Shucks, Homer, what can happen from playing a record?" Freddy demanded. "All that can happen is it can sound awful, or something like that, and we can be ready to put our hands over our ears, just in case."

Homer still looked doubtful, so Freddy said, "Grownups are always funny like that, anyway, Homer. You know that! They tell you not to listen to murders on the radio, and then give you a radio for Christmas. They tell you not to read comics, and they sell 'em like hotcakes. The sixth-grade teacher says, 'No gentleman chews bubble gum,' and her old man sells about a hundred sticks a day in his candy store. I don't see why you should be *afraid* to play—"

"I'm *not* afraid to play it!" Homer interrupted hotly, because his pride had been hurt. He jammed his hand into his pocket and jerked out his nickel. Then he marched straight up to the jukebox, poked one of the buttons, *the button,* the one without a name, and jammed his nickel into the slot.

There was a loud *cl-l-lick!* and mysteriously and silently the disgustingly unbreakable record slid out of the stack and began to spin. Both Homer and Freddy watched out of the corners of their eyes, wondering what kind of a weird noise, or music, or even a scream might come blaring out of the jukebox. They stood poised, hands ready to clap over their ears, prepared to dash out of the door.

As the music began flowing out of the jukebox they sighed with relief and began to smile. It was only a gay little tune with a bouncing rhythm!

"That's sure a surprise!" said Homer, happily changing colors and nodding his head in time with the music.

"There's nothing wrong with that music!" said Freddy, beginning to tap his foot. "Golly, that's a catchy tune!"

After a few more measures of the catchy rhythm, a song began coming out of the jukebox:

> "Sing hi-diddle-diddle,
> For a silly little vittle.
> Sing get-gat-gittle,
> Got a hole in the middle.
> Sing dough-de-dough-dough,
> There's dough, you know.
> There's not no nuts
> In you-know-whats.
> In a whole doughnut
> There's a nice whole hole.

When you take a big bite,

Hold the whole hole tight.

  If a little bit bitten,

  Or a great bit bitten,

Any whole hole with a hole bitten in it,

Is a holey whole hole

And it JUST—PLAIN—ISN'T!"

After a few final measures of the catchy music the record stopped playing. Freddy cried, "That's about the best tune I've ever heard, Homer, and the words are sort of good too. I'm gonna play that record *again!*"

Freddy deposited his nickel in the jukebox, and once more he and Homer nodded and tapped time to the tricky music and listened to the tricky words. Before the song was halfway through they were singing gaily along with the voice coming from the jukebox—

"In a whole doughnut

  There's a nice whole hole.

When you take a big bite,

Hold the whole hole tight.

  If a little bit bitten,

  Or a great bit bitten,

Any whole hole with a hole bitten in it,

Is a holey whole hole

And it JUST—PLAIN—ISN'T!"

"There just plain isn't anything wrong with that record," said Homer.

"Na-aw!" said Freddy. "The guy was nuts! Like you-know-whats!" Freddy giggled and hummed a few measures of the catchy tune.

"I could sit around," said Homer, "for a holey whole day and not do a thing but listen to it play."

"Say, Homer," said Freddy, starting to laugh, "do you-know-whats? You're talking a little vittle bit funny!"

"Hawh!" Homer grinned at Freddy. "You're talking *notes,* just like *music,* and a little bit bitten funny too!"

"That's not nut-nothing," Freddy started to sing, "to get-gat-gittle excited about."

"No, not a bit bitten," Homer agreed.

"Not a little bit bitten," Freddy sang.

"Or a great bit bitten," Homer joined in.

"And any whole hole with a hole bitten in it, is a holey whole hole and it JUST PLAIN ISN'T!" They ended up singing as loud as they could sing and stamping time with their feet.

"That was just plain swell!" Freddy sang happily when they had finished.

"But, Freddy," Homer sang sadly, "we're a little bit bitten!"

"Or a great bit b——" Freddy stopped singing suddenly, and the smile faded slowly from his face. *"Holey whole holy smoke!"* he sang forte-forte.

"Yes, holey whole holy smoke," Homer encored in a pathetic piano-piano.

The barber put down the cards he had been dealing to Uncle Ulysses, Posty Pratt, and the mayor. He answered the telephone, listened for a minute, and then called over his shoulder, "Pipe down for a minute, you guys. Got a bad connection or something. Oh, Homer, it's you," he said, finally recognizing Homer's voice.

"Yes, he's here. I'll call him to the phone." He jerked his thumb at Ulysses. "Homer is on the line. Says you better get-gat-gittle back to the lunchroom. Funny thing," the barber continued, "sounds just as though he were *singing!*"

"Hello, Homer," said Uncle Ulysses. "What? What? What's that you're singin'?" He listened attentively for a while and then asked anxiously, "But the *jukebox* stops playin' and singin', doesn't it? Oh, well," said Uncle Ulysses soothingly as he regained his smile, "that's nothing to worry a bit bitten about. For a minute I thought that the *jukebox* couldn't stop! Say, Homer, that's a good number you're singin'," Uncle Ulysses said. "Sing it just once more, please, from the beginning."

Uncle Ulysses, with the receiver pressed tight to his ear, stood swaying and tapping time with one foot, then with two feet, and then he started singing:

"In a whole doughnut
There's a nice whole hole.
When you take a big bite,
Hold the whole hole tight.
If a little bit bitten
Or a great bit bitten,
Any whole hole with a hole bitten in it,
Is a holey whole hole
And it JUST—PLAIN—ISN'T!"

"Thank you, Homer, that was just plain swell!" Uncle Ulysses

complimented with a cadenza. Then he sang "Good-by!" and turned to the barber, the mayor, and Posty Pratt, singing, "Drop your cards and get all set, this song is swell for a male quartet!"

And it certainly was a swell song for a male quartet! After about three practice tries they rendered it in perfect four-part harmony. They sang it a little bit bitten better every time they sang it the holey whole hole way through. By the time that Uncle Ulysses and Posty Pratt discovered that they could not stop singing first and second tenor, and the mayor and the barber discovered that they could not stop singing alto and bass, they had already set a non-stop record for barbershop quarteting.

Finally four desperate men burst out of the barbershop, in the closest of close harmony, and went singing off in all directions.

When Uncle Ulysses came high-diddle-diddling through the door of the lunchroom he created a minor discord, until he started singing in the same key as Homer and Freddy and about two dozen or so after-the-movie customers. The customers, when they had first arrived in the lunchroom, had been very much taken by the charming little melody with the clever words that Homer and Freddy kept singing over and over again. One by one they too had joined in, and one by one they too had discovered that they could *not stop* singing the charming little melody with the clever words.

The soprano from the church choir was hitting A flat above high C and giving out with a get-gat-gittle that made every piece of glassware in the lunchroom vibrate and tingle. She was being well supported with dough-de-dough-dough from a full mixed chorus of male and female voices of all ages, not to mention all colors, thanks to the jukebox and its tastefully contrived lights.

Never, no, never before had there been such a gay and carefree, downright enchanting song being sung by such a puzzled, downright unhappy gathering of people.

Homer was singing and singing, along with everybody else in the lunchroom. He was trying and trying, along with everybody else, to forget the clever words and the charming little melody. He tried singing another song, "Mary had a little vittle!" and couldn't get-gat-gittle past the very first line before he was right back dough-de-dough-doughing at the very top of his lungs.

He looked anxiously around him at the faces of some of the more experienced singers, the soprano, the deacon, the dentist, and Uncle Ulysses, all people who had been singing for years and years and could be more or less depended upon to sing in the proper key. They could always be depended upon to stop when they came to the end of the song too. But not tonight! Tonight they couldn't even slow down, let alone stop!

"What if we *never* stop!" Homer began to worry. "Somebody has to think of a cure," he thought, so he began to think just as hard as his poor young song- and rhythm-racked mind could think. He remembered that something like this had happened to him once before. It was last September, when he had read a verse in a library book and couldn't stop repeating it. He remembered that there was a cure in the story. Now if he could only recall the name of that book, or the name of that story! Several times during the past hour he had been ever so close to remembering, but then suddenly he was caught up again in the catchy rhythm of the jukebox song.

Homer looked at the clock and saw that it was five minutes of nine. In five minutes the library would close for two weeks!

172

"We just got to find that book right away!" Homer thought. "We just got to get-gat-gittle that book from the library, no matter what!"

He waited for a moment, until the soprano finished off a particularly high and ear-piercing passage, then jumped up on the counter and soloed, "Every-body follow me-e-e, over to the librar-re-e-e!"

The soprano, having the loudest voice, spoke or rather sang for the entire group, "We will follow Homer Price, he can help us, ain't that nice?"

And they all danced out of the door after Homer, singing:

> ". . . hi-diddle-diddle,
> For a silly little vittle.
> Sing get-gat-gittle,
> Got a hole in the middle.
> Sing dough-de-dough-dough,
> There's dough, you know.
> There's not no nuts
> In you-know-whats.
>
> In a whole doughnut
> There's a nice whole hole.
> When you take a big bite
> Hold the whole hole tight.
> If a little bit bitten,
> Or a great bit bitten,

Any whole hole with a hole bitten in it,

Is a holey whole hole

And it JUST—PLAIN—ISN'T!"

It was closing time, and the librarian had just finished counting thirty-one pennies in fines from overdue books. She glanced quickly around the library to see if there was any last minute thing to attend to before she locked the door and went off on her vacation. She glanced thoughtfully down the neat shelves of books. Then she looked at the carefully stacked periodicals and

made a quick mental note to renew the subscription to the *Musical Monthly* as soon as she returned. Then she closed the big dictionary that Freddy had left open, so dust would not settle on the page of "Ps" during the next two weeks. At last everything was neat as a pin. Every chair and table was placed just so, and every last book was resting in its proper place, on its proper shelf.

"Now," she thought happily, "I can go on my vacation. *This* is the moment I have been waiting for!"

And *that* was the moment that Homer danced diddledy-viddledy in through the vestibule and *crash!* tripped over the standing sign that said "Quiet, please."

The soprano hit high A flat right on the nose as she fell on top of him, followed by a mixed quartet, a trio, a couple of septets, a few odd stray singers, and Freddy, who had not had much previous musical experience.

Before this heap of melody had untangled itself completely, the mayor crescendoed into Uncle Ulysses' well-padded musical coda. Then the judge, a couple of city councilmen, and the dog warden sang in next, all dancing in an appropriate dignified manner.

Posty Pratt sang his way in at the head of his family of wife, daughters, sons-in-law, eight grandchildren, and an elderly second cousin of Mrs. Pratt's, who was having herself a high old time keeping time with her cane.

Homer wiggled to his feet and danced straight for the librarian. "We're a little bit bitten!" he sang. And the entire group chorused, "A little bit bitten, or a great bit bitten . . ." They sang the whole song for her, better than they had ever sung it. It really did sound wonderful, and it certainly showed what a little practice can accomplish.

The librarian could not help but be impressed with such beautiful singing, but after listening to three or four renditions she began to worry about catching her train and tried to ease people politely toward the door. When she began to have an irresistible urge to sing too, she began to understand the unhappy predicament of all of these forlorn souls who were singing such a gay and carefree little song.

"What can I do to help?" whimpered the librarian, trying her utmost not to sing the question.

"There's a book here on the shelves that'll tell us how to cure ourselves," Homer soloed.

"What's the title?" yelled the librarian, losing complete control of her library manner. "Do you know the author's name? What's the book's catalogue number?" she screamed.

"Dough-de-dough-dough, I do not know," sang Homer. "Those things I cannot remember, but I read it last September."

"Then there's nothing I can do, get-gat-gittle, I can't help you," the librarian chanted, beginning to be a wee bit bitten herself.

"We have to find a black-backed book, or maybe it's a brown-backed book," sang Homer. "And I think it was a little bit battered!"

Then everybody, the poor librarian included, joined in singing, "Find a black-backed book that's a little bit battered, or a brown-backed book that's a little bit battered." And at the same time everybody, the poor librarian included, started dancing past the shelves, snatching out every single brown-backed and black-backed book they came to.

". . . dough-de-dough-dough,
There's dough, you know.
There's not no nuts
In you-know-whats!"

They all sang as they danced back and forth and in and out among the shelves of books. They started carrying an endless stream of brown-backed and black-backed books to where Homer was dancing and singing on the largest reading-room table. To most of these, which were the wrong shade of brown, or too thin, or too fat, or too battered, or too new, he just sang, "No!" or shook his head in time with the music. The books that Homer rejected were tossed in a disorderly heap that brought tears to the eyes, and a sob to the contralto voice, of the librarian.

Any books that looked about right as to size, color, or amount of battering, Homer quickly thumbed through, to see if he could find the story that he was sure would cure them of their terrible affliction.

"In a whole doughnut there's a nice whole hole," everybody was singing and singing and then singing some more. The volume would gradually diminish as voices tired, and then someone's eye would light on a letter "O," or a number "800," and burst out with a loud *"Holey whole hole!"* and that was enough to set everybody off at full blast again. They just couldn't stop singing the silly song. The more they sang, the more they danced past the shelves; the more they danced past the shelves, the more books they collected; and before very long Homer was perched in the middle of a tremendous pile of brown-backed and black-backed books that were a little bit battered, more or less.

There were books of art and biography, history and literature, philosophy, geography, geology, philology, zoology, and even economics, but Homer still hadn't found the book that he re-membered reading last September. He courageously kept on looking, and everybody else kept on singing and dancing past the shelves, and bringing more and more books.

Freddy started dancing precariously along the balcony, and books started sailing over the railing to Homer, who caught them expertly to the tune of "High-diddle-diddle, for a silly little vittle," without skipping a single beat in the rhythm.

Suddenly the books that Freddy was lobbing from the balcony started sailing right on past Homer, because Homer was giving his undivided attention to a story in a slightly battered brown-backed book.

Almost before you could sing "Tom Robinson" everybody had gathered in a rhythmically swaying group around the base of the mountainous pile of books.

"Looky-look-look, it's a brown-backed book," sang the weary soprano.

"Get-gat-gittle, he's got a story in the middle," Uncle Ulysses sang hopefully in his tired tenor.

Suddenly Homer stopped swaying and bobbing. He smiled and kept reading, and then he started to sway and bob again. But while everybody else was swaying, Homer was bob-bobbing, and when the others bobbed, Homer swayed. Homer was caught by a *new* rhythm all his own. Then from the top of the pile of books he began to shout at the top of his voice:

"Conductor, when you receive a fare,
Punch in the presence of the passenjare!
A blue-trip slip for an eight-cent fare,
A buff-trip slip for a six-cent fare,
A pink-trip slip for three-cent fare,
Punch in the presence of the passenjare!

CHORUS

Punch, brothers, punch with care!
Punch in the presence of the passenjare!"

Before Homer started shouting the second chorus of "Punch, brothers, punch with care!" the singers began to falter in their rhythm for the first time that evening. Then one by one they began to shout along with Homer, "A pink-trip slip for a three-cent fare," until everybody, yes, everybody, began to stamp his tired feet for joy and shout, "Punch, brothers, punch with care! Punch in the presence of the passenjare!"

That is, everybody except Homer. He sat smiling and out of breath on his perch atop the pile of books.

Everybody else was yelling, *"Punch, brothers, punch!"* and stamping so hard that the chandelier shook. The few red and blue and yellow books that remained on the shelves shook, even the "Quiet, please" sign shook and rocked on its legs to the rhythm of the stamping. But not Homer. Homer was cured.

After he had rested for a moment and caught his breath, he slid unobserved down the pile of books.

"A blue-trip slip for an eight-cent fare!" Everybody was shouting and stamping so loud and so hard that Homer was completely ignored. He dodged expertly through the group without being stamped on, receiving only a light unintentional clip from the cane of Mrs. Pratt's elderly second cousin.

Homer needed somebody to help complete the cure—anybody who had not yet heard the "Punch, brothers, punch" jingle. He rushed out of the door to bring back the very first person he should meet.

The chances were one hundred and two to one that it wouldn't be the person it was—there were at least one hundred and two Centerburg citizens who were not inside the library, but there she was, coming right up the library steps. It was the *sixth-grade teacher!*

"What has happened to Lucy?" she cried, referring to the librarian. "It's almost train time!"

"You've got to help," Homer said. "Come inside so they can tell you."

As they came in through the door Homer shouted as he had never shouted before. "Tell it to her!" he bellowed, pointing to the sixth-grade teacher.

And they told her:

"Punch, brothers, punch with care!
Punch in the presence of the passenjare!"

They very generously told her two times, all the way through, without holding back a single "Punch" or "Pink-trip slip."

Like all sixth-grade teachers, she was very quick to catch on—caught it good and perfect:

"A blue-trip slip for an eight-cent fare,
  A buff-trip slip for a six-cent fare,
  A pink-trip slip for a three-cent fare,
  Punch in the presence of the passenjare!"

Then, as suddenly as they had started shouting and stamping out the jingle, everybody stopped, just as Homer knew they would—everybody, that is, except the sixth-grade teacher. She'd caught it just too perfect, and she went right on shouting and stamping. Everybody else sat down, gasping for breath, right where they were, to rest their tired and aching feet.

Freddy, being young, recovered his wind quickly and edged his way over to where Homer stood.

"Now, what," he asked, nodding at the howling, stamping sixth-grade teacher, "are we going to do with *her?*"

"She'll be all right," Homer said confidently, "as soon as she tells it to somebody else. Just like I was cured when I told it to you, and you were cured when you told it to her."

"You mean to tell me that after you tell that jingle to somebody you forget it and are cured?" Freddy asked.

"Yep, that's the way it goes," said Homer, "just like in the book."

Freddy thought for a moment and then asked, "And the person she tells it to has to tell it to somebody else?"

"Yep, Freddy, somebody's *always* gonna be saying it," Homer admitted.

"Gets to be monotonous, doesn't it, Homer?" Freddy commented, shaking his head sadly toward the sixth-grade teacher, who was just beginning another chorus. "It will be terrible to have to listen to somebody around town keep on saying and saying that jingle forever and ever!"

"That will be better than having everybody in Centerburg keep on *singing* forever and ever," Homer argued. "And besides," he continued, "she's going on a vacation, isn't she? We'll just have to make sure that she gets on that train without telling somebody, and all our troubles will be over! C'mon, Freddy, we gotta get busy."

The two boys went around rousing everybody, making them put on their shoes, and explaining what had to be done about the poor teacher.

The mayor acted at once. While lacing his shoes, he appointed a committee of the two councilmen and the dog warden to collect baggage and to see the librarian and the teacher to the train.

Everybody filed out of the library. The librarian turned out the lights on the still swaying chandelier and locked the door on the shambles of her Dewey Decimal System. She helped lead the helplessly reciting teacher to a waiting car, and they were whisked away to catch the train.

"Golly, Uncle Ulysses," Homer said, suddenly remembering, "nobody has been looking after the lunchroom for a whole hour!"

"By jingo!" Uncle Ulysses snapped his fingers. "You'd better run right on back there, Homer. I've got a little matter to talk over with the barber and the mayor. Are you coming too, Posty?" he asked the postmaster.

Mrs. Pratt frowned, and Posty sheepishly said, "No," and marched away home at the head of his family.

Uncle Ulysses, the barber, and the mayor headed for the barbershop, and the soprano and all the others walked off on their tired and aching feet.

"We were awfully lucky, Homer, that somebody hadn't borrowed that book from the library," Freddy said as they settled down once more with their books. "We'd be singing yet!"

Homer nodded thoughtfully and didn't answer.

"What's the name of that book?" Freddy demanded.

"It's a book of stories by Mark Twain," Homer replied. "He's the same guy that wrote *Tom Sawyer,* and *Life on the Mississippi,* and a lot of other good stories."

"It's sure a good book to know about," Freddy commented. "In case you ever need it again, you know just what to ask for. Say, Homer, how did that jingle go?"

"I can't remember, Freddy," Homer said. "That's the kind of jingle it is—you can't stop saying it until you tell it to somebody else, and then you forget all about it. I wish I'd thought to write the jingle down on a piece of paper and keep it handy. It's like you said, Freddy, a guy might need a jingle like that in a terrible hurry some time, and it could save an awful lot of trouble."

"I'll help you copy it, Homer," Freddy offered, "just as soon as the librarian gets back from Yellowstone Park."

"Why, hello, Sheriff," Homer greeted as the sheriff walked in the door. "Where have *you* been all evening?" he asked, remembering that the sheriff had not been a part of the strange singing and reciting.

"Over to the state capital," the sheriff said, nodding his greetings. "I was attending a meeting. I'm hungry, Homer. How about a cup of coffee and a piece of apple pie?"

"Sure thing, Sheriff," Homer said. "Freddy, you start some fresh coffee while I get the pie."

Both boys were hustling around behind the counter when they heard a *cl-l-lick!* that made their hair stand on end. When they

turned, there was the sheriff, all grass green and smiling, standing next to the jukebox with his coin purse still in his hand.

"What one are you playing?" Freddy yelled, making a quick end run around the counter to look.

"It's—it's—" said Freddy in a terrified voice as he watched the disgustingly unbreakable record slide out of the stack.

Then Freddy sighed with relief and changed to a brighter shade of lavender as the magic-like machinery quickly and silently flipped the record over.

"Golly, that was a close call!" cried Freddy. "For a moment I thought—"

Then a gay and lilting little melody began pouring out of the jukebox.

"That's nighty mice music," the sheriff said, beginning to nod in time with the melody.

And then the song began flowing out:

> "A *hip*-high *hip*popotamus
> Said, '*Hips* and lips make most of us.
> From tip to tip a five-foot lip,
> From *hip* to tip a three-foot foot.
> With three-foot feet,
> Our four feet meet
> The ground, so we won't tip a bit.
> I bet you never yet have met
> A tippy, lippy, *hip*-high *hip*popotamus.' "

"Homer," Freddy gulped, "we got to get hold of that book— the one by the guy that wrote *Tom Sawyer* and *Life on the Mississ*—"

"Aht, aht, aht, aht!" Homer interrupted violently. *"Don't say Mississi*—the name of that river!"

Then he right away, fast as he could, filled two glasses with water. The two boys solemnly held their breath and counted to ten and drank the water down.

"There!" said Freddy, smiling once more, "that always cures

my *hi*—makes them go away. I guess the whole thing was just our imaginations, eh, Homer?"

"Yeah, Freddy," said Homer, "we must have just dreamed the whole thing." Then, as the music coming from the jukebox ended with a spasmodic chord, Homer turned to the sheriff and said, "Sheriff, here's your piece of *hip* pie."